THE NIGHT CIRCUS

and other stories

T0160144

THE NIGHT CIRCUS

and other stories

Uršuľa Kovalyk

Translated from the Slovak
by Julia and Peter Sherwood

PARTHIAN

**CYNGOR LLYFRAU CYMRU
WELSH BOOKS COUNCIL**

Co-funded by the Creative Europe Programme of
the European Union

Published with the financial support of the Welsh Books Council
and the SLOLIA Committee, the Centre for Information on
Literature in Bratislava, Slovakia

Uršuľa Kovalyk is a poet, fiction writer, playwright and social worker. She was born in 1969 in Košice, eastern Slovakia, and currently lives in the capital, Bratislava. She has worked for a women's non-profit focusing on women's rights and currently works for the NGO Against the Current, which helps homeless people. She is the director of the Theatre With No Home, which works with homeless and disabled actors. She has published the short story collections, *Neverné ženy neznášajú vajíčka* (*Unfaithful Women Lay No Eggs*, 2002) and *Travesty šou* (*Travesty Show*, 2004), and two novels, *Žena zo sekáča* (*The Second-hand Woman,* 2008) and *Krasojazdkyňa* (*The Equestrienne,* originally published in Slovak in 2013 and in English by Parthian in 2016) which was shortlisted for Slovakia's most prestigious literary prize, the Anasoft Litera Award, and received the Bibliotéka Prize for 2013. Her most recent collection of short stories, *Čisté zviera (A Pure Animal),* appeared in 2018.

Julia Sherwood was born and grew up in Bratislava, Slovakia, and worked for Amnesty International in London for over twenty years. **Peter Sherwood** taught Hungarian at the School of Slavonic and East European Studies (now part of University College London) and the University of North Carolina at Chapel Hill. They are based in London and work as freelance translators from and into English, Slovak, Czech, Hungarian, Polish and Russian. Their book-length translations include Peter Krištúfek's *House of the Deaf Man* (2014) and Uršuľa Kovalyk's *The Equestrienne* (2016) for Parthian, as well as works by Balla, Béla Hamvas, Hamid Ismailov, Daniela Kapitáňová, Hubert Klimko-Dobrzaniecki, Petra Procházková, Noémi Szécsi, Antal Szerb, Miklós Vámos, and Pavel Vilikovský.

For more information, see juliaandpetersherwood.com

Parthian, Cardigan SA43 1ED
www.parthianbooks.com
First published in 2019
© Uršuľa Kovalyk 2019
© This translation by Julia and Peter Sherwood
An expanded version of the Slovak collection Travesty šou (ASPEKT, Bratislava, 2004), incorporating three stories from the collection Čisté zviera (Pure Animal, Divadlo bez domova, 2018) and one story that has not been published in book form, The Night Circus and Other Stories has been translated into English by Julia and Peter Sherwood.
ISBN 978-1-912681-04-4
Editor: Carly Holmes
Cover design: Syncopated Pandemonium
Cover image: Lucia Dovičáková www.dovicakova.com
Author photo: Patrik Krebs
Typeset by Elaine Sharples
Printed by 4edge Limited, UK
Published with the financial support of the Welsh Books Council and SLOLIA, the Centre for Information on Literature in Bratislava, Slovakia
Co-funded by the Creative Europe Programme of the European Union
British Library Cataloguing in Publication Data
A cataloguing record for this book is available from the British Library.

Contents

Predator

The air smells of melting plastic. The red of the traffic lights is shimmering in the sun. The car wheezes as if about to give up the ghost. "It's an old banger," says Paula, picking up on the thoughts in my head. The old banger emits a ferocious rattle, as if warning me not to insult it so brazenly. The temperature in the car keeps rising as Paula licks her ice cream languidly and her luminous red hair drives me to distraction, a red rag to a bull. I just can't tear my eyes away from it.

"That hair of yours is going to blind me one of these days," I say, winding the car window down. Paula tosses her red mane and bares her teeth at me flirtatiously. A predator, I think. Not even a corpse could resist Paula's sex appeal. She isn't all that young or beautiful, nor even particularly fit, but every time I see her I'm ensnared by her charm, like a fly falling into a pot of honey. I try to puzzle out what it is that makes her so attractive. It must be her velvety voice or perhaps those taut blue veins on her beautiful neck that put me in this wicked frame of mind. Whatever. Paula is a friend of mine and I'm not in the habit of sleeping with my friends… In fact, generally speaking, I'm not even attracted to women, except that Paula is not a woman, she's the quintessence of sex and it makes no difference what gender you are; she would seduce a sexless fly. She's a hunter, she has never let a man pick her up – she's always been the one who chose her men and she would always get the one she wanted. A predator.

"And still I've ended up with the wrong one," says Paula, interrupting my thoughts.

"Are you a mind-reader now?" I blush.

"No, but I can read it in your eyes, they can't lie."

The lights change and I manage to start up the old banger again. A fresh breeze streams in through the open windows, cheering us up. I turn off onto the road leading out of town. "Really, Paula, how could you have got it so wrong?" I smile and sing naah na-na-na-naah, out of tune.

"But he's not so bad, really," she intones. "Or bad-looking," I respond.

"But… I really don't know why the word 'but' keeps cropping up in my life, I might as well have it carved on my gravestone, right after Rest In Peace: R.I.P. but…" adds Paula, biting into her ice cream cone. Her teeth make a crunching noise, like a cat crushing the frail bones of a bird. Quite a predator! I steer the Skoda around a bend. The tyres screech. "You ran over a corpse," jokes Paula and I make a gesture that suggests she should stick it up hers.

"D'you know what a woman feels in bed after twenty years of marriage?" she asks, shooting me the hottest glance ever. "No," I say, swallowing hard. "Nothing," Paula frowns, shaking the crumbs off her dress. "And that's the point – nothing. Sometimes when we're having sex I'm aware of every single move and sigh my husband makes, I keep track of the fridge whirring, I hear my neighbour yelling at her kids. I watch the stains on the white wall – the other day I thought I saw a face there. I try to think of something sexy, like this young shop assistant or a film scene with two women making love to a man beneath an enormous silk scarf. Still nothing. Nothing at all. And this nothing is eating me up, the void is getting so colossal it feels like someone has blasted a huge hole in my stomach. With a machine gun. And if by some chance he asks how I'm feeling, I can't find words to describe how I feel. Nothing. A perfect Nothing."

"So you've discovered Nothing in lovemaking," I say, trying to make Paula laugh, while she is lost in thought and chews her lower lip, plump like an overripe raspberry.

There is a young hitchhiker standing by the roadside and Paula is so taken by his long blond curls that she tells me to stop.

He tries to explain in broken English where he's headed. Only when he swears do I realise that he's Hungarian. We discuss where we are headed and where he needs to go, and I torture my tongue with my kitchen Hungarian. "Don't worry, Paula, we'll give him a lift," I reassure her as I notice the alarmed expression on her face. "A little present for you, you'll have half an hour to admire him, then he gets out."

Paula gives a laugh and her voice takes on the timbre of the darkest night; her entire body turns moist and supple so that I half expect her to melt on the passenger seat like ice cream. She's just gorgeous. She licks her lips and her blazing eyes burn through the young man's face. A predator. Ready to leap. I strain my kitchen Hungarian to get some small talk going but the old banger makes such a racket nobody can make out a word. Paula is in raptures, she gushes over his shirt, saying how nice it is, but it's just a pretext to touch his shoulder.

"Paula, control yourself, can't you see he's just a puppy." I'm trying to tame the tigress, ready to pounce. "Should we get him laid?" she shouts over the whirring of the car. "Wouldn't that be something? We could just turn off into the woods and seduce him."

"No, Paula, that would kill him." I stop her in her tracks and she purses her lips like a little girl, winking at me and doing her best to stop me from being a spoilsport and to make me go off into the woods. I laugh and so does the young man. Perhaps he's figured out what's going on.

I put on some music to drown out the noise of the engine, some loud rock that makes Paula bounce about and almost sets her seat on fire. "Go on, ask him if he fancies me." Paula gives me a prod with her elbow. So I use my broken Hungarian again to ask, but the young man is reticent. "He says you're extremely beautiful, like a goddess, but he's got a girlfriend and is head over heels in love with her, you know," I translate for Paula.

"Aaah," she says, disappointed. She calms down a bit. The music and the noise of the Skoda are about to burst our eardrums and Paula keeps mum, devouring the young man with her eyes. "Look at his gorgeous skin," she says admiringly, "and that cute little bum. I'm sure with him I wouldn't need to play a film scene in my head or look for faces on the wall."

"Oh I don't know, Paula, maybe you need an affair," I reply.

"You know the problem with affairs? After a while they start resembling marriage. Ten years ago I had an affair. It was brilliant for a year but then I was spending a weekend at this guy's place and instead of flinging me on the kitchen table and making passionate love to me he asked if I was going to make something for dinner. So I said, Do I look like a cook to you? Like I'm your wife?" Paula says, raising her eyebrows and lighting a cigarette. "That pissed him off," she says, exhaling, "he said I was a nymphomaniac, can you believe it? If you want to screw you're a nymphomaniac, if you don't, you're frigid. I've never been able to find the golden mean my husband keeps going on about."

"Because it doesn't exist," I chip in, smiling at the hitchhiker. "The golden mean for you might be totally over the top for someone else," I say, winding down the car window all the way.

"I guess the problem is that my husband's pheromones don't seem to be working anymore because on my fertile days I feel like I'm on fire, I'm randy all the time, you know, but he doesn't feel like it. Once he said he was scared that I was going to rape him, he says that it turns him on when I'm submissive, passive, when I'm just lying there with my legs spread wide, waiting for my dear hubby to give it to me and then say: Thank you, Sir!"

I laugh; the thought of a passive Paula waiting for her man strikes me as rather funny. "So why on earth did he marry you, surely you've always been like this?" I ask.

"Yeah, we talked about that, too. I asked him straight out what made

4

him fall in love with me to begin with and you know what he said? He said I reminded him of his mother, can you believe it? No way! He *really* likes his mother, see? I was so pissed off that I asked him why he didn't go and fuck his mother!" declares Paula, putting out her cigarette and checking her cleavage.

"And what did he say?" I ask.

"He said I was insensitive, that I have a sick imagination and that I should see a sex therapist, that ever since we got married I've been fighting his mother but that I would never live up to her standards because she's a woman with a capital 'W'," she says, spitting it all out in a single breath, her chest heaving with the torrent of words.

"Oh, so you're a woman with a small 'w'?" I tease Paula.

"I'm a woman with a huge clitoris, that's also something he once said to me: Your clitoris is so huge, it's not normal! I was so livid that I flung a lamp at him," she adds angrily and red spots appear on her neck.

"Really, Paula, it's about time you did something about that clit of yours, it's hanging out of your skirt," I keep teasing her and she starts laughing like mad. She slaps her thighs and covers her mouth in a rather theatrical gesture. "Yeah, that's it, I always make sure that it hangs down to the floor so I can use it as a mop!" she adds. But I notice that in the back seat the smile has frozen on the young man's face. I suspect the word for clitoris might be the same in Hungarian.

"I've never passed judgement on his tool, never ever, because I don't care about that, as long as he is deft with his fingers," Paula holds forth, furiously tossing her red mane. "But for him it's a matter of pride, that dick of his. Even though it's not his erection that turns me on, it's something quite different, you understand?" she asks, looking at me to check that I do understand, but just at that moment the young man asks me to pull over, and says he's getting out. He smiles, casting fearful glances at Paula.

I let him out at a petrol station. He says thank you. "What a cutie,"

Paula sighs, sadly stroking my thigh. She waves at him from the open window and shouts *veesont latashra*, goodbye in Hungarian, in an atrocious accent.

Paula watches the road for a while. Tiny flies quietly die on the windshield after colliding with the car. "Or that time when I was breastfeeding my daughter," she continues, "I had loads of milk and when I came it would squirt all over the place. And do you know what he did? He told me to keep my bra on the next time because he found it revolting!" She drags out the word 'revolting' so that it ends up sounding like the drone of my car. "Can you believe it?" she insists, waving her arms in front of me. "My breasts produce food for his child, I feel literally like a milk cow, and he informs me that he finds it revolting."

"What did you throw at him? Admit it," I interrogate her.

"Nothing at the time, I just locked myself in the bathroom and had a cry."

"Bathrooms have a charm of their own," I remark with a sigh.

"They're a good place to cry," Paula nods, lost in thought. "Well, and after that I always kept my bra on, but looking at those parachutes made me feel like all sorts of things except sex."

The sun has stopped beating down, and the silvery surface of a lake comes into view through the front windshield, which is starting to look like an insect graveyard. Departing holidaymakers hoot their horns. Tyres kick up dust on the road. "I haven't brought my swimming costume," says Paula, "we'll have to find a spot that's tucked away, somewhere I can go skinny dipping."

"Since when have you been so bashful?" I ask her as I park. She doesn't answer, staring longingly at the surface of the water. I take the towels from the boot and we start walking along the shore hoping to find a secluded spot so that Paula could, as she puts it, give her abnormal clitoris a nice bath. After half an hour we find a tree shading a small bay that is deserted apart from some cans and empty beer bottles. Paula undresses. She discards her dress, her bra, then hesitates a little before taking off her knickers. "Should I go in starkers?" she wonders. "Go on, there's nobody here," I say and also start to undress.

Paula dives into the water like a killer whale, splashing about and turning every which way. "I love water," she squeals. Her huge white breasts glow on the surface like lamps, bouncing as she kicks at the drifting algae. I want to go in but the water is too cold. I stand on the shore and hesitate. Paula mocks me, calls me an ice princess and a couch potato.

"Look, Paula, there's a bag floating on the water next to you," I shout. Paula looks around and curses the idiot who threw the plastic bag into the water. I let her be for a while, then wind her up again. "Oh, now I see, it's your clit!" I shout. She gives me a nasty look and tells me I'm horrible. She laughs and splashes me. The sun is tiny, like a dot of red ink in my son's exercise book; fluffy cotton wool falls into the lake from the cottonwood trees and Paula does the season's first handstand in the water. The skin on her thighs glistens in the last rays of the setting sun and the curls on her vagina look like matted sealskin. I take a deep breath and do a belly flop into the water.

Rainy Day Joe

I found him one morning when I went to take out the rubbish. He lay in the grass, clutching a piece of dirty plastic in his tiny baby hands. His eyes were closed and he didn't seem to be breathing. His crumpled clothes were strangely fluorescent. As if shiny fish were swimming around them. He was as light as a feather and gave only a quiet sigh when I picked him up. Back at home I wrapped him in a blanket and poured gallons of hot tea down his throat. It took ages for him to open his eyes.

He looked like a child or a dwarf. In short, like a creature from another world.

He never told me who he was or where he'd come from. And I couldn't pronounce his name properly; it sounded a bit like Joe, but with a lisp. He had big sad eyes that kept changing colour, from a pink tint in the morning, turning to dark green and then to a dark ochre as the day went on.

He spoke in a weird lisping voice. It sounded like the rustling of a paper bag. I taught him to talk, use cutlery and flush the toilet after use. He loved stewed cherries. And on long rainy nights, as we lay naked on a multicoloured rug, he caressed my body with a bit of sheep fur. He stared at everything in amazement, opening those huge eyes wide, and so did I.

I was fascinated by his masculine yet tiny body, his perfectly formed buttocks and beautifully shaped feet. They never smelled.

After lovemaking I watched him as he slept. His curly eyelashes fluttered with the rhythm of his dream. Like runaway horses. He loved to dance in a white ballerina dress I bought him. He looked like a lovely dancing sprite. He never reproached me about anything, never harassed me and never yelled at me. Our relationship was like a chance encounter that was repeated on a daily basis. And every day amazed us anew.

He was frightened of storms. When it was pouring outside, he would stand by the window, raise his finger and lisp, "Joe mushn't get shoaked!" And I would say, "Don't worry, darling, I'll buy you an umbrella, as big as a giant burdock leaf." That made Joe laugh. When he laughed he made me forget all about reality and lies.

We never left the house except to go to the front garden, and only on sunny days at that, when there wasn't a cloud in the sky and the wind dispelled Joe's fear of rain.

Gold-coloured leaves floated down from the trees, and he would glue them to my body. A velvet-pawed kitten he had brought home was our breakfast companion. And the thin trail of honey I licked off his thighs in the evenings seemed never to end.

One day Joe and I were rolling about in red paint on a huge sheet of drawing paper. The doorbell rang and I found my ex-boyfriend at the door. We hadn't seen each other for a year. Long enough that it didn't bother me. In no time at all, before I knew it, he was inside the house, a bottle in his hand and a broad grin on his face. "I just wanted to see you," he exclaimed, planting a long kiss on my cheek.

I staggered back and fumbled with my red hands to close my towelling robe, from which a breast was popping out.

"This is Joe," I said, pointing to the little red man parading around my room naked. Joe had never been shy but when he saw a huge man stare at him in astonishment he went to fetch his ballerina dress, just in case.

"This is Eduard," I said to him. Joe stood in front of Eduard, his mouth open wide, admiring the hand Eduard had reached out to him.

"Wow, he is sho big!" Joe chirruped.

"Eduard is my ex," I added but Joe just raised his beautiful eyes, still pink at this time of the day, and said, "He's enormoush."

We sat down at the table. Eduard opened the bottle and while Joe went to clean up, he asked with a sneer, "Don't tell me this is your new boyfriend?"

I snapped back, "Yes, he's my new boyfriend and he's from Iceland."

"Come on, he's got a lisp and he's just a tiny dwarf," Eduard taunted me, pouring himself some wine.

"Look, Eduard, you would also have a lisp if you spoke Icelandic and It doesn't matter that some people are small and others big. Now tell me, what is it that you want?"

Eduard came up with every cliché in the book, from how lovely I looked, to how hard his life was and eventually blurted out that he needed somewhere to crash for two weeks.

That day didn't end well. Joe made friends with Eduard, who got him drunk. Joe spent the whole night throwing up into a bucket by the bed and laughing out loud. And Eduard stayed.

Suddenly everything was different. The house was full of Eduard; he filled the whole place, my fridge was cluttered with beer cans, wherever I moved I would trip over his stuff and I had to listen to his booming voice. He gave me a headache. His jokes drove me mad and the way he fumbled with his fork made me want to bite his hand off. But what hurt me most was seeing Joe change. He was enraptured by Eduard, following his every step and imitating everything he did.

Eduard took advantage of this, of course, and taught him everything he thought a real man ought to know. And I mean everything: from spitting down from the balcony to swearwords, which he claimed would come in handy at football games. Joe no longer wanted to wear ballerina dresses. He made me buy him the kind of clothes Eduard wore. And once he put on trousers and a baseball T-shirt he looked like an ordinary, tiny, ridiculous man. No longer like a creature from another world. His face coarsened, he drank beer and spent all day watching TV with Eduard. He no longer danced. And he didn't amaze me any longer either. From time to time he would still cuddle up to my tummy, looking over his shoulder to check that Eduard couldn't see him. Meanwhile I was counting the days. Two weeks. It had to come to an end.

However, two days before he left, Eduard had the brilliant idea of taking Joe to the pub, for a kind of stag party. That devil, Eduard. Outside it was raining cats and dogs. Raindrops sang a gurgling song in the drains. Joe hesitated for a moment, while I raised my finger and reminded him that he mustn't get wet. But Eduard slapped him on the back and said he had an umbrella and that he shouldn't be a wimp and scared of rain. Joe gave me a wink and followed Eduard out into the dismal weather. Before they had got too far from the gate the wind turned Joe's umbrella inside out and I could see through the misted-up windowpane that the rain hit him right in the face. I heard Joe's lisping scream. He threw the umbrella away and thin, candyfloss-like threads began to unravel from his body. I ran out of the house. Joe began to dissolve. Quietly, like when a paper handkerchief drops out of your pocket and the rain turns it into a translucent sugar cube. His face began to disappear. I tried to drag him back but all I was left with was his clothes and those limpid emerald-green eyes, fluttering like wounded butterflies.

Eduard left. The devil. Now I spend long rainy days sitting in a white ballerina dress, writing about the day I took out the rubbish and found a creature clutching a piece of dirty plastic.

The Dog in the Fridge

I woke up in a place I didn't recognise. It wasn't my flat, my bed or my bed linen. I found myself lying in the middle of a vast empty room, white as fog, with polished floors and no lamps or electric sockets. There were no windows and the only door opened into a kitchen. I got up and tiptoed around the room. My feet didn't make a sound on the floor. The kitchen wasn't really a kitchen either; it had no cooker, no fitted cupboards, no sink. It was as white as the other room, and the only piece of furniture was a fridge. It was an Electrolux and the lights on its huge door twinkled like those of a spaceship. It stood in the corner of the room, completely silent, and the electric cable emerging from its bowels disappeared somewhere into the distance. I opened the fridge. There weren't any shelves, boxes or an egg tray. It was crammed full of meat. Animal feed, I guessed. Strewn about the floor were chopped off thighs, blood-red lungs, tails, a big purple tongue, ribs and... a dog. A white dog with black spots around his eyes. The spitting image of the dogs you see in vintage photographs, the kind that sit on a cushion with a kitten between their paws. I touched it. It was as cold as all the other meat. It was ice-cold. Like the fridge. Nevertheless, it opened its eyes and looked at me. It wagged its tail and shivered like bees struck by spring hail. It tried to smile but its lips managed only a frozen sneer. It seemed to be resigned to lying there and didn't even try to get out. A freezing dog, I thought, and slammed the fridge door shut.

The fridge flashed its lights like a spaceship and it began to multiply exponentially. Both rooms were now filled with flashing, softly whirring fridges. I went from one room to another, opening the fridges. All were crammed full of frozen meat but the dog was nowhere to be seen. I rummaged through piles of lungs and dug my fingers into bone-hard thighs, breaking my fingernails. Where are you? I yelled, but the only response was chilly silence. I kept opening fridge after fridge but couldn't find the dog anywhere.

My knees started to tremble in panic and cold sweat trickled down my back. The thought that I would never find the dog again made me compress my lips into a thin line. The idea that I would never be able to let it out of the fridge made me gasp for air. Where are you? I yelled again. Like a stack of cards, the fridges collapsed into a single one.

I opened it. It was completely empty. No dog or meat. Just the cold white surface. I walked in.

Cold enveloped me. It felt as if my entire body had been smothered in a coolant emulsion. I found myself standing in a huge room that opened into a hallway. The hallway was blue, a cold blue like the coldest sky in Antarctica. I kept walking. The hallway was full of shiny little tubes and droning compressors, and the frozen liquid formed a thin layer of ice on the floor. I slipped. I crashed into a wall and my nose started bleeding. The blood turned into a thousand tiny red balls, all rolling unstoppably in one direction, as if pulled by some unknown force. I ran after the little balls. They led me to a gigantic kennel, totally white with a little red heart on the front wall, a bit like dog kennels in the countryside. It was there, tied to the kennel. The dog. It was still cold but there was now more spring to its movements and I saw it was trying to tear itself free of the coarse rope that was strangling its neck. The dog kept tugging away but the cold rope seemed frozen solid to its skin. I started looking for scissors or a knife but all the pockets on my pyjamas were sewn up. I broke down in tears. I chewed on the rope, scratched at it with my fingernails, spat on it to loosen it. Freezing fog began to pour out of the compressor, becoming ever thicker. My muscles were getting stiff, my toes were turning purple. And the dog yowled. I was frightened that we would freeze to death, that I would never manage to untie the rope, that we would stay in the fridge forever. Like the meat. Animal feed.

I must get some hot water, I thought. My mum always used hot water to defrost the fridge. I tried to collect enough saliva in my mouth and wondered how on earth I could get hold of hot water in this fridge.

As the first drops of hot urine started to flow, my hands were the first to warm up. I strained to make as much liquid as possible spurt out of my body. The urine made a hissing noise as it came into contact with the frozen rope. At first the yellow vapour stung my eyes. The rope began to soften. It started to yield, melting like ice cream in the sun. The dog was free. The minute the rope eased off its neck we found ourselves outside the fridge.

The room was still completely white but now I was beginning to make out delicate patterns on the walls, little Braille-like bumps forming flowers and sea-shells, butterfly wings and giant trees. My eyes slowly followed lines that resembled men, women and children. The more I touched the walls the more pronounced the lines became. I realised they were all coming together, melding into endless stories.

The dog sniffed at me. Its coat acquired the sheen of white coffee. It lay on the floor contentedly, steam rising from its mouth. I noticed a small white handle on the right-hand side of the wall. I pushed it. The dog ran up to my feet, wagging its tail. A door suddenly appeared in the wall and opened wide. On the other side I saw my room, my bed with its rumpled blankets and pillows, my clothes and favourite books. The sun came streaming through the windows. The stuffy smell of a room just waking up made my knees tremble. I looked into the dog's eyes. It held my stare, looking straight back at me. Intently, as if trying to tell me something. As if trying to instil in me the idea that had kept it alive in the fridge. My scratched fingers began to sting.

The appeal of the room's smell was irresistible. Come, I said, and the dog gracefully leapt onto the blue carpet, sniffing it. Then it started running around the room. While I turned the radio on and made some hot coffee it made a wet patch on the carpet. I gave it a stern look. The dog sat there scratching itself behind the ears, yelping happily.

Red Shoes

I've kept them. Stowed them away on the top shelf. Where there's no dust. Where nobody can see them, Few people can reach that high. I don't know where they came from. I must have been born wearing them. Maybe I came by them as my mother struggled in labour, just as the obstetrician's metal scissors cut into her puffed up vagina, accidentally brushing against my tiny, mucous head as it was pushing its way out. Just for a split second. The cold metal reverberated on the skin. Like a saw touching a sheet of paper.

Snip. My brain was preparing for the birth, ready to instruct my lungs to draw breath and my vocal cords to emit a scream. And suddenly, snip. Metal. Cold, since nobody thought of warming it up. Something snapped in my head. Metal. Like a damaged diskette. Not completely, just enough to erase the information. With a pair of scissors. Their coldness. Their sharpness. Instead of calm. A pair of shoes. Shoes that leap into darkness instead of walking. They were invisible at first. They had not yet acquired the garish colour that would later hurt the eye. Invisible, they slept inside baby blankets, prams and strollers. In order to grow. In order to let my feet grow stronger and my heels harden.

How many years did they need before they reached the right size, the red shoes? Ten years, maybe fifteen? Before I became fully aware of them, they were already a shiny, dazzling red. Red like blood. Like spilled wine. They held my feet tight, keeping them firmly on the ground that would start rocking again and again. They kept me safe.

My red shoes. They acted like a magnet, like a weight. The invisible, still point of my universe. But you know what they're like, red shoes. They're too unruly. They have a life of their own. Before long they started to drag me around. Along roads leading nowhere or straight to hell. Across abominable dirty swamps full of demons and death. In and out of sex. In and out of love. They tested me to see how much I could take. Whether I could take it. It never occurred to me to ask them to stop. I was their slave. Their instrument. They knew what I desired. Always. No sooner would an idea or an image start forming in my brain than off they would go in hot pursuit. Always knowing the right direction. Taking short cuts, of course. Insane, rough short cuts that nearly gouged out my eyes. I would reach my destination half-blind, only to be forced to keep going on and on.

They made me dance when I couldn't take it anymore. Like that time.

It was an ordinary, dismal summer day. People had sweated off all their dirt. They stank, leaving behind huge puddles of sweat. I jumped over them. I trusted the shoes. That day was so dismal, so ordinary it made me want to cry. I leapt over a tram lazily dispatching sun-drunk people to their destinations. Even the clouds in the sky were devoid of charm. They looked like scraps of paper. Or rags scattered on the ground. My shoes were the only things gleaming. I was besotted with them. It never occurred to me that I should not obey them. And that's how it happened that on that dismal, god-awfully ordinary day, as I recalled the face of a man I had dreamt of the night before, they went "hop".

Hop is an easy word. So easy it's hard to believe that a single word could have propelled me. Right into his flat. Into his bed. Into his hands and his… The man I saw in a dream. He said there was no need to take my shoes off. I think he did it on purpose. He noticed what kind of shoes I was wearing. Had I taken my shoes off in the hallway like a good girl, maybe I might have felt the whiff of death emanating from his skin. Maybe. But I'm not a good girl and the little red riding hoods on my feet took a short cut straight into his.

I felt like it. Felt like dancing a little. Just like that. Like jumping up and down on his white bed linen in my red shoes for a while. Until the open bottles of wine started to rattle. The soles of the shoes, too, were on fire. I could hear them hissing. I laughed. Those red shoes are a load of laughs. They don't know how to tread seriously. The man said… Fuck.

Fuck is a complex word. I don't know what it means exactly. Whether it's meant as an insult, a swearword, an expression of desire or astonishment. So I waited to hear what he would say next. Surely you can't begin and end a sentence with a single word. You're not going to finish your sentence? I asked. It was a sentence, right? I enquired, intoxicated by the shoes, disgusted by the ordinariness of the sun. But the man stood his ground, I guess men always do. He started skinning my neck. The way you shuck sweetcorn. The way you pull meat off an overcooked duck. As if he wanted to tear my body into tiny pieces. The first message that reached my brain said: it hurts. I tried to explain that I just wanted to have a little dance and that this was no reason to hurt me, that I really had to go, ouch, ouch! He wouldn't take no for an answer. And as my neck started to swell, like a twisted ankle or a skin eruption that had got infected, I realised he was about to kill me. Fuck. It's such a complex word. It didn't occur to me that it could also mean to kill. Because of my red shoes. Out of envy.

I couldn't let him skin me completely, until there was just a bare skeleton left that he would toss out of the window. A skeleton wearing red shoes wouldn't look right. So I kicked him. The way one kicks a dog on heat. In the neck, where his Adam's apple was going up and down. It was a very precise kick. Thanks to the shoes. I kicked him with all my might. I kicked him hard. I kicked him so that he would understand that I wasn't going to take no for an answer cither. I kicked him again and again. I went on kicking him like there was no tomorrow. My feet fired off arrows, lances, weapons of every kind. As

I kept kicking out, the red shoes turned into two jumping red blotches that glued his eyes together. He went blind for a moment. For a while it was like floating in space in slow motion. I felt carried away by the shoes. I could feel them running, leaving a black mark on the lino. I heard them wheeze and shriek. Bristling cats. Red-eyed cats. They ran fast. Like seven-league boots.

That was the first time I took them off. Standing in front of the mirror. Feeling my purple neck. And realising it really was purple.

Purple doesn't suit me. It makes me look cadaverous. The shoes were dangerous. Wearing them made me dangerous. I took them off and put them away. They wept. They begged. I tucked them away on the top shelf of the wardrobe, where no one can reach them. Where there's no dust. But I have kept them. I hardly ever wear them. Only when you're not looking. When the full moon slices the countryside like a silver wheel. When the earth begins to sway beneath my feet and I start losing my way. That's when I jump onto a chair. It's so simple. Up I leap onto a chair. I put them on. I polish them. They glow red, lighting up the room. I go wandering about but only when the moon is full. I visit unhappy weddings. Burnt-out marriages. Non-existent lovers. My solitude. Whenever I dance on top of the table I run the risk that the shoes will sweep something off the table. Empty words. Knives of obligations. Your perfectly-baked idea of me. Cutting it into pieces. So that a new idea can be born. It might be better or worse, but it's always new. I'm keeping them.

So that I don't forget. So that I don't lose my mind out of boredom. Just for a day or two. Never longer. I wear them to bed. I kick you away in my sleep. My sense of freedom grows with every kick. I like leaving and coming back. To find myself. Find myself again. Is that a bad habit? Like biting one's fingernails? Every time I visit a lonely woman I check the top shelf of her wardrobe. Where there's no dust. Where they are asleep. A fixed point in the universe. A mad point in the universe. The unruly red shoes.

The Moon Maiden

It is midnight. A round moon shines through the half-drawn blinds. It lights up the room taking care not to wake anyone. It transforms the dust on the old furniture into golden sand. Marta is not asleep. She has been waiting a long time for the house to go quiet, to go to sleep, for her husband's and children's regular breathing to drown out the last sound. Nothing but the creaking of floorboards, the sound of a wardrobe slamming shut somewhere, and the ticking of the clock, disrupts the reign of sleep. Silence. There's no sound from the street either, only the clanking hand on the broken clock in the square measuring out the night.

Marta stays in bed for a while, quietly following the ray of moonlight. Then she gets up and soundlessly walks over to the other room. She sits down in an armchair, pulling her knees right up to her chin. She embraces her bare heels. It is quiet and dark. Marta loves the silence. After an entire day filled to the brim with thinking, rushing and talking, she can finally muse on all the trifles in the world. The trifles of her world. Sometimes it doesn't work. She falls asleep, exhausted, before her body even touches the bed. Today she has managed to do it. She's alone at last. Alone with herself. Her eyes rove around the furniture, the knick-knacks, cupboards and rugs. The room looks different at night. The night blunts sharp edges, transforming rough materials into velvet. Even the grand piano, which Marta really hates because it's in the way and she keeps having to polish it, has been transformed into a raven's black wing. Marta likes ravens. They remind her of the night. They remind her of silence.

The moon moves, rolling on to another part of the sky. A sharp band of light cuts through the room. Like scissors, she thinks. She puts her hand inside it. In the light her hand turns translucent, smooth, moon-like. The cracked skin is gone. What a beautiful hand, thinks Marta, and dips her other hand in the light. She twists and turns it around for a while, observing the beads of sweat that have turned silvery. Marta is sitting in the armchair. It is dark. Everyone is asleep, the room is silent. She is sitting in the armchair, the band of light enfolding her hands. She enjoys it. She starts moving her hands as if washing them. Gradually, she dips her toes, her knee and a breast in the light. Then her elbows, belly and shoulders. She bathes her whole body in the moon's white light.

Marta stands up and quietly fetches a mirror. She picks it up and immerses her face in the light as well. It is yellow-white, somewhat silvery. All her wrinkles have gone, and so have all her birthmarks and spots. Her skin is smooth and translucent. Perfect. Like a skull. She bares her teeth and sticks out her tongue. "Moon maiden," says Marta. The woman in the mirror repeats the words.

The moon moves on again. It rolls over. It tumbles over like an orange ball on a black carpet. The light hits the wall. It licks a picture. It's an old picture. Marta has forgotten all about it. It's been a long time since she looked at the pictures on the wall. It's a photograph, actually. It shows a little boy carrying a fish on his head. He's standing on the seashore. The sea is grey. She cut it out when she was still young, from some magazine. She forgets which. But now the moon has illuminated the boy. The huge fish on his head glistens. Marta looks into his eyes. How can he be carrying such a huge fish? And for so many years. On his head. She examines his scrawny body, torn clothes and bare feet buried in sand. His lips are chapped from the sun. The fish's eye stares dully at the sky. Suddenly the boy moves. Slowly turning his head, he scratches his knee and puts the fish down on the ground. "Marta," he says, "my fish is hungry." Startled, Marta opens her mouth. She can't believe what she's seeing. It's just a picture, she tells herself, but she moves closer to take a better look at the fish.

Sure enough, the fish looks emaciated, its ribs protruding from under its skin. Its huge gaping jaws are silently gasping for air. "I've forgotten," Marta says. "I've long forgotten." The boy rolls the fish over. Sand sticks to its thin body. Slowly, the fish's eye begins to move. It looks at Marta. "Your fish really is hungry," she says and picks it up. The fish is light, like a sheet of paper. Like a dried-up leaf. Her little finger feels the faint beating of its cold heart. She caresses it, steeping it in the narrow band of light, kisses it. She puts it to her face. She swings it to and fro, cuddling it and patting it. She sings to it. The fish grows. Its body becomes rounder, its skin more supple, the ribs begin to disappear and its eyes regain their proper fish-like lustre. Before long the fish is flapping about in the white moonlight. "Moon maiden," the boy says. It is quiet. Everyone is asleep.

The moon maiden stands in the middle of the room holding the flapping fish. She hands it back to the picture. The boy smiles. He smiles and flings the fish into the sea. He's now standing alone, his feet buried in the sand. Somewhere in the distance there's the sound of the murmuring sea. The moon rolls over to the far side of the sky. All of a sudden it's dark. The band of light disappears and the raven wing turns into a black hole. For a long time Marta stays standing in the dark in front of the picture on the wall. She examines it keenly. The boy remains silent. Only his big brooding eyes stare into the darkness. Marta feels relieved. She goes to bed.

The morning is different. Mornings are always different. They're filled with restlessness, shouting, laughter. The children get dressed, yelling and fighting. They bang the doors. Marta prepares breakfast. She serves hot toast. The kettle is steaming. The butter is melting, everyone takes their seats at the table. Her husband munches on his toast. Crumbs come flying from his mouth, the children bicker. Their hands draw greasy maps on the table top. They poke each other in the ribs, ask questions non-stop. It makes her dizzy and her hands start trembling. She's not really hungry. She gets up and walks over to the other room to fetch a shirt for her husband.

The room looks different in the morning. The raven wing has gone, the furniture is covered in ordinary dust. The outlines of the chairs are sharp. She glances at the picture. A little boy is standing in the sand on the seashore. Marta opens the wardrobe. The smell of clean laundry caresses her nose. "Marta," her husband says, "it's time." He points to his watch. She hands him his shirt. "Have you noticed?" she asks. Her husband puts on his shirt, the fragrance clings to his body. "Noticed what?" he says, doing up his buttons with his fingers, thin as a spider's legs.

"The boy in the picture isn't carrying a fish on his head anymore," she says. His eyes wander towards the picture. "There's never been a fish on his head, Marta," her husband replies. Marta is taken aback. For a brief moment she hesitates. But then she remembers the mirror, the moon maiden. The narrow band of light. "There was, last night," she says. She sounds confident. "It was on his head," she tells her husband, looking him straight in the eye and holding his chin. "And the fish was hungry, so I fed it and then the boy flung it back into the sea. That's why it's not on his head anymore."

Marta keeps looking into his eyes. Her husband stops doing up his buttons. He goes up to the picture incredulously. "You must have been dreaming," he says, wiping some dust off the picture frame. "I felt its ribs in my hands and its heartbeat in my little finger," she adds stubbornly. Her husband sighs. Marta sighs too.

"I've got to go, it's getting late," says her husband, hurriedly putting on his tie. He slips his coat on. He picks up his keys. The children run to the car. Marta watches from the window as they argue about who will take which seat. They pull off each other's hats and kick each another. Her husband shouts at them. They go quiet. The car flashes its rear lights. By way of goodbye.

Marta walks around the rooms that now seem alien to her. She takes in the mess throughout the house. Piles of underwear strewn about. Scraps of paper. Bits of chewing gum stuck to the furniture. Hidden screams. Piles of questions and future answers. Before she gets to work she makes herself a cup of coffee. She sits down in the armchair in front of the picture. She puts her feet up on the coffee table. The boy stays silent. Marta sips her coffee. And somewhere deep in the sea a glistening fish is swimming round and round.

Suicide

After I committed suicide in my bathroom on 8 May at four in the morning, my soul slipped out of my body like a bar of wet soap from the hands of a clumsy child. In my dying ears the dripping tap sounded like a metal rod hitting the railing at the entrance to our block. I wanted to stay there and keep looking at my white body lying in the bloodied water but the force pulling me upwards was stronger. I found myself in front of a white wall without doors, translucent like the jelly topping on my mother's Sunday cake. I was completely alone. There were no angels, no glowing light, no God. No forgiveness. Only a long, never-ending wall. I touched it. The wall moved the way transparent deep-sea creatures move. It turned into a white canvas that showed my own reflection. I screamed. The echo of my voice bounced off the wall, hitting me in the face sharply like a tennis ball. A film started rolling, grabbing me by the throat. It was the film of my life.

I see my mother in labour, my head pushing through the warm interior of her vagina, my eyes blinded by too many lights and a male voice echoing among the greenish tiles announcing that I was female. My bottom is slapped repeatedly, I bawl. Next I feel myself sucking warm milk from my mother's breast criss-crossed with blue veins, I defecate and lie in my pram watching the leaves dance on the trees. My parents' cheerful faces appear accompanied by the rays of the setting sun. The film accelerates. I am now standing by the wall sticking my fingers into a socket. My mother screams, a slap on my wrist frightens me, her angry mouth tells me I mustn't be naughty. Just obedient. Just nice and pretty. I'm standing in front of a birthday cake, thousands of candles glimmering in the dark, my fringe almost catching fire. Everyone claps and tells me what a sweetie I am.

At my mother's command I sing, dance and recite poems, I swirl around, passed from one hand to the next. Like a trained monkey. I stand in front of a mirror trying out a cigarette. In the morning my mother pulls my hair weaving it into complicated plaits. I cry. She says you have to suffer for beauty. I see myself walking to school along a road covered with fallen leaves, the wind blowing and my feet in pink tights growing numb. The lady in the kiosk tells me I look like a sugar doll. I see my mother drunk, throwing up in the toilet, and my father having sex with a neighbour. There are piles of bottles everywhere. A friend of my father's strokes my bum. Every sweet he gives me adds to my sense of guilt. The film rolls on. I'm sitting at the table, it's Sunday lunch and the cutlery clinking against the plates is the only sound slicing through the silence. I say I feel unhappy. Mother says: How come, you're so pretty. Father shakes his head and tells me not to be so silly... They make sure I'm wearing the right expression and the right clothes.

The film winds on faster, I'm fifteen and get my first period, Mum says I mustn't tell anyone about it, I'm to pretend I'm just fine. The pain pierces my belly, I'm on the toilet inserting the sanitary pad in my knickers the wrong way round. I'm sitting in my father's room again, he strokes my thighs mumbling that I'm almost a woman now. The extra money he gives me disgusts me. Mum catches us in the act, she slaps my face. She screams that it's all my fault. I'm standing in front of the mirror trying out Mum's make-up, I smear foundation on my face and blood-red lipstick on my lips, my mum's voice ringing inside my head. You must make sure you always look your best.

The film keeps speeding up. I'm at school. I'm scared of the other girls who talk back, and suck up to the teachers. I flirt with the PE teacher, ratting on the girls who smoke in the toilets, I swipe the most expensive tops from Mum's wardrobe. My classmates hate me. I always try to look my best. I stuff myself with the birthday cake before Mum takes it away so that I don't get fat.

The film keeps rolling faster and faster. I spend the evenings crying and secretly stuffing myself with chocolate. I keep going to Dad's room. Mum buys me a slimming diet book. I don't have a single friend. I'm alone. The film on the wall suddenly acquires a pink hue. I'm at the bar in the student hall of residence. I notice you for the first time, you're sipping a fragrant coffee. You ask me what I'll have and I don't know how to make small talk. I feel my legs trembling. I'm aware of you picking me up with your patronising smile and undressing me with your eyes.

The film slows down, now it has more of a reddish tint. We're sitting on a bed and you are kissing me. It feels as if you're trying to bite all the birthmarks out of my body. I don't feel like making love but you take me by the neck and your hand, which brooks no resistance, undoes your flies. Oh yes you do, you say and I feel you thrusting your hard, hot penis into me. I lie back. Like a rag doll. While your hips pump away at my hips in a motion familiar from Dad's porn videos. You're not taking any notice of me. I try to look into your eyes. I have only a bit part in this play. Your sweat burns my thighs, your penis cuts me like a birthday cake. My mother's voice is ringing inside my head. You've got to look your best. Scream, she tells me, but I can't produce a sound.

But that's not the end of the film. The bubble turns into a huge fisheye magnifying the picture, and I see your penis delving deep into my vagina in slow motion, rubbing it, tearing it, every move sending thousands of microscopic skin particles flying. The film gets jammed and restarts, it goes around in a loop, endlessly repeating the image of my vagina stuffed full of your penis. It is suffocating. The scraps of skin fly about like snow. I throw up.

I return into my body, sliding in like a bar of slippery soap into a child's hands, and the metallic sound, like someone hitting the house railing with an iron rod, pierces my eardrums. The water is cold.

The Bathroom

Ágnes Mickievič wasn't an alcoholic. She had never had more than a single glass of wine, not even at her aunt's wake even though a distant cousin spent the whole night trying to entice her to drink more. Mrs Mickievič never took any medication, she had no idea what marijuana was and her only information on psychotropic substances came from spine-chilling stories on one of the three channels she could get on her old TV. Mrs Mickievič was sixty, and she and her husband, Mr Mickievič, a pale fellow who suffered from allergies, lived in a grey prefab block of flats. Her life was identical to those of many women her age, women whose youth had been spent under the shadow of the Iron Curtain and who had wasted their prime in queues for bananas. It was a life without ups or downs, without passion or direction, without emotional outbursts or love affairs. It resembled the never-ending knitting of scarves for the winter, one's daily grooming, doing the washing up or taking out the rubbish. It resembled every kind of uninspiring activity except life. Mrs Mickievič wasn't unhappy; she just took life for granted as something inevitable, like cold rain in October or sleet in December. She didn't yearn for change because she could not imagine it, and the well-trodden track of her daily married life offered her serenity and certainty of which, as she used to say, one could never have enough in this hectic world of ours. Her marriage to Mr Mickievič was... well, it just was. Their relationship, their whole way of life, had all the appearance of a safe haven finally reached by ships after the storms of youth on the raging seas. Except there had never been any storms.

31

The Mickieviĉes' flat was in their image. Neither too large nor too small, it was frugally equipped with useful objects such as a vacuum cleaner, a food processor and lamps. Austere objects of simple shape and undistinguished colour. You wouldn't find a single unnecessary knick-knack on a bookshelf; everything served a purpose and even if it didn't, Mr Mickieviĉ would promptly find some use for it. For example, they were about to throw away a long bamboo stick he had been given by his colleagues, a useless thing, Mrs Mickieviĉ said, until Mr Mickieviĉ had the idea of using it to close the curtain that kept getting stuck. The sole justification for having furniture – chairs, the mirror, even the worn armchair – was for them to sit on it, store their clothes in it or apply cream in front of it, but it had never even occurred to them to buy anything just for fun. The Mickieviĉes' flat was free of paintings, rugs, statuettes or plants. And because of Mr Mickieviĉ's allergy you wouldn't find any tablecloths or doilies on the tables and the total number of cushions (hypoallergenic, of course) amounted to two.

So, although sixty years of age, Mrs Mickieviĉ was not an alcoholic. Mr Mickieviĉ never drank either, he had never been a gambler or skirt-chaser, and he had never raised his hand to his wife, which is quite rare in this part of the world. He had married her because he happened to come across her and appreciated her practical sense as a unique quality sorely lacking in other women. Mrs Mickieviĉ accepted his proposal in order to get away from home. The number of siblings at home far exceeded the capacity of their undersized flat and since she couldn't stand a mess or unnecessary talk, she agreed to put on an impractical frilly white dress and suffer the indignity of the so-called "ride" dance at the wedding party. Mrs Mickieviĉ wasn't in love with her husband. She had read somewhere that love was undesirable and since it had never happened to her, she regarded it as yet another impractical silly thing, invented by people out of boredom. She had never wanted children, because children are messy, she didn't own a dog because they can't be milked, she didn't grow geraniums because they don't yield apples. The first thought that went through her head whenever she came across something new was – what use could one make of it? Thus the Mickieviĉes had spent many years living together as the sole pair of an extinct species of animal, the last of its kind, and this feeling bound them together more tightly than sex, money or love ever could.

Since Mrs Mickieviĉ had never taken any medication, not even painkillers, what happened to her one night took her by complete surprise. It was quite late, though not yet the middle of the night. Mr Mickieviĉ had already gone to bed and she was still up, comfortably seated in the capacious armchair, knitting a waistcoat for his sensitive lower back. The lamp threw a yellow light on her rhythmical purl-stitch and her wedding ring, the only adornment on her hands, and glowing little flames onto the polished chest of drawers. She didn't feel like going to bed. She felt unusually lively for this time of day and so she just said good night to her husband and he asked her to be careful not to wake him when she came to bed, for he was a light sleeper, as she knew. As she did her knitting, Mrs Mickieviĉ wondered what the waistcoat would look like, imagined Mr Mickieviĉ wearing it under the winter coat they had bought the year before so that he wouldn't catch a cold, which would ensure she wouldn't have to rub that disgusting, smelly ointment onto his back.

As her eyes wandered from the knitting needles to the furniture, making sure everything was in the right place, she noticed light coming through a crack under the bathroom door. She was annoyed to think that Mr Mickieviĉ had forgotten to turn the light off, something that had never happened before, and thought that he must be getting old and she would have to have words with him. She put down her knitting and went over to the light switch. However, she found it was in the right position, so she flicked it up and down a few times to check if it was working. But the light didn't go off and she noticed there was a greenish tinge to it, translucent and fresh like a pond overgrown with weeds that she used to see in the countryside as a child. Cautiously she opened the door. And having never tried psychotropic substances Mrs Mickievič was completely taken aback by what she saw in the bathroom. The shiny white tiles, as well as the washbasin, bathtub and the transparent shower curtain, had vanished and were replaced by a lush green rainforest, complete with trees, lianas and the fleshy moist leaves of some exotic plants she had once seen in an encyclopaedia. Instead of the lino, the beautiful lino she and her husband had bought two years ago, there was black soil on the floor, covered with rotting leaves with colourful insects crawling across them. Mrs Mickievič was astonished by the scent that hit her nose, it was moist and sweetish, smelling of… cinnamon, was it? And so heavy she had to take a deep breath to check that there really was air in her lungs.

The fragrance overwhelmed her, seduced her, relaxing her neck muscles, stiff from knitting, titillating and unsettling her, until Mrs Mickievič caught herself with one foot ready to step into the fluorescent greenness. She paused in surprise. What use is it? she thought, and grabbed hold of the doorjamb to steady herself. Quite useless! And since she could see no practical purpose in their bathroom turning into a tropical forest, she stood in the doorway, hand over mouth, examining the huge lake that had appeared where the bathtub used to be. She was a bit frightened. Yes, frightened. In her mother's family there had been the odd case of madness, schizophrenia or obsessive-compulsive disorder in the shape of an aunt screaming nonsense and taking her knickers off in public. I must have got it now, she thought as she watched a giant butterfly flutter its shimmering wings on a cyclamen-coloured flower. She slammed the door shut although the noise was quite faint compared with the thumping of her heart, which seemed about to leap out of her chest, and she ran straight into the bedroom to lie down next to Mr Mickievič whose regular breathing filled the room with calm.

That night Mrs. Mickievič didn't put her knitting away, she didn't change into her nightie and, more importantly, she couldn't go to sleep. She lay stiffly by her husband, listening to the sounds that were now audibly emanating from the bathroom. Or rather, from what used to be the bathroom. There was the strange shrieking of animals, chirping of crickets and singing of birds, all swollen into one rhythm, like an orchestra playing, with one part starting up as soon as another died down. Mrs Mickievič went on listening to the orchestra almost until dawn, when tiredness made her close her eyes and she sank into the sweet forgetfulness of sleep that featured no bathrooms or tropical forests. In the morning Mr Mickievič spotted the mess in the form of the sloppily discarded knitting, noticed that Mrs Mickievič had gone to bed without getting changed, as well as the huge bags that had appeared under her eyes. He asked if she was ill. Ágnes Mickievič just shook her head and shuddered at the thought of what would happen once Mr Mickievič made his way to the bathroom, as he did every day. But the rain forest was gone. The bathroom had turned back into an ordinary bathroom with its clean lino, redolent of the smell of antiseptic detergents, exactly the same clean, austerely and practically furnished bathroom that they had been using day in, day out, for years.

Even though Mrs Mickievič had never taken any medications before, this morning she swallowed nearly half a tub of headache pills. Her husband was surprised but not enough to bother opening his mouth and stop doing his breakfast crossword. It was Saturday and their flat exuded calm, as it always did. Mr Mickievič did his crossword puzzle and sipped linden tea while Mrs Mickievič pottered about the kitchen, preparing chicken with almond stuffing, her great-grandmother's recipe, for lunch. Confused thoughts of the bathroom and the rainforest she had seen the night before coursed through her head. She wondered if some dormant gene had awakened inside her, the same one that had landed her aunt in a psychiatric clinic. She had visited her in hospital and as she recalled the impressions of handcuffs on her aunt's wrists, she decided not to mention her experience to anyone. After all, the rainforest was gone so what would be the point of telling anybody about it. The chicken stuffing turned out to be a great success again. So did the stuffed peppers Mrs Mickievič cooked in advance for the next day, and so did the sponge cake she baked, as well as all the other dishes she prepared in the course of the following week, forgetting all about the bathroom.

She cleaned the bathroom at the same regular intervals as before, once a week, donning yellow rubber gloves, and she would have gone on cleaning it regularly until the end of her life had it not been for a distant relative of Mr Mickievič's dying somewhere in Moravia. She had met the relative and had received a wonderful quince jelly recipe from her. That was why she neatly packed her husband's suitcase and walked him to the station when he set off for the funeral.

That night Ágnes Mickievič was all alone. She put her feet up on an old ottoman and relaxed, letting her glasses slip off her nose. She began to nod off. The flickering blue light of the TV screen cast slightly ghostly shadows across Mrs Mickievič's face. She awoke to the chirping of crickets. This was so powerful that it drowned out the comedy programme for pensioners on the TV; it sounded like a rattle or cowbells, and kept swelling until it became so unbearably loud it made Mrs Mickievič get up from her armchair. She was drenched in sweat. The bathroom was again glowing green, exuding a magical light like a lamp that attracts moths. The light mingled with the shrieking of monkeys, the screeching of birds and the drumming of water as it dripped onto the leaves. Oh no, not again! thought Mrs Mickievič and as if hypnotised started walking towards the bathroom door that stood wide open, the smell of the rainforest even more intoxicating than the last time.

She paused in the doorway. She held on to the brown doorframe, her fingers gripping it with all their might. She was determined not to step inside, not to let the sick gene come to the fore, not to fall for this, not to succumb; to resist, to withstand… She was determined, but not wholly. Somewhere deep inside her, behind her lowest rib, a tiny part of the soul she never knew she had started to peel off. And once the tiny flaking part of her soul caught the smell of the blossoming liana, it peeled off her body. Smack. Like a moistened stamp coming off a white envelope. And Ágnes Mickievič's soul entered.

There were giant ferns, screeching mandrills, guerezas, resplendent toucans and thick snakes. As thick as the trunks of trees whose branches formed an emerald curtain above Ágnes' soul. Her soul was light. It was semi-transparent but soon it acquired the colour of the forest and, unencumbered by her body, it didn't have to be careful not to squash the polka-dot-covered beetles it stepped on. It moved about soundlessly like a thought. It expanded like a fragrance. It undulated like fog, rippling in the morning breeze. It sparkled like a wet leaf chanced upon by a ray of sun. It flowed like a river, drilled its way through like a caterpillar, it flickered like the iris of a jaguar's eye. It was not a visitor here. It was an integral part of the rainforest, as if it had always belonged there, long before it was born in the body of Mrs Mickievič, the wife of Mr Mickievič. She was alive. She was truly alive. She didn't know how long it lasted. The bark of the trees she rubbed against wiped her clear of all sense of time. She didn't wake up until the sun came out and ordinary life clattered all around her and she had to massage her cheek, sore from the hard doorframe. While Mr Mickievič was away for the first time in ages, she visited the rainforest every night for a whole week.

When her husband came home, Ágnes could smell the sweetish smell of death on his clothes. She thought it strange because, though she had attended many funerals, she had never smelled death before. Mr Mickievič sank exhausted into their one huge armchair and, as usual, asked Mrs Mickievič for a cup of linden tea. She made it for him as usual, letting the dried linden blossoms brew for the required length of time. Nevertheless Mr Mickievič did notice his wife's creased clothes, the magazines strewn carelessly all over the floor, the unwashed dishes and the grease spots on the bathroom lino. He realised something wasn't quite right. Even though Ágnes was behaving as usual, he sensed a kind of distractedness in her behaviour and her voice, noticed the absent look in her eyes when she looked at him, and her indifference to things she normally found irritating. He wasn't stupid. All of a sudden something was different, something he couldn't put his finger on but he eventually put it down to hormonal changes in Ágnes' body, typical of women her age.

The Mickievičes' bathroom was no longer the Mickievičes' bathroom. It belonged to Ágnes. It had turned into the realm of her soul that was peeling off her body in ever thicker layers, a realm where she could wander about, feeling and smelling, a world without detergents, filled with wondrous flowers which would have been sure to trigger Mr Mickievič's allergy and which, until recently, she had regarded as quite unnecessary. The infinite rainforest that by now spread its branches in her bathroom every night, enticed her to keep walking deeper and deeper into it, letting her peeled off soul discover hidden caves overgrown with moist moss, the uncanny faces of statues of black stone and paths whose ends she could not see. The only living things Mrs Mickievič's soul encountered in the jungle were animals that never ran away from her, who didn't seem to see her, so that she was able to examine at close quarters the patterns on the plumage of a bird or the blurred spots on a predator's velvet body. And even though Mrs Mickievič had never encountered a single human being on her wanderings, she knew that somebody was there, living somewhere in there, indeed watching her from behind the green-hued leaves, and that it was only a matter of time before she came across this person. As if that somebody were calling to her. At night she thought she heard a voice, an incomprehensible whispering, an insistent, guttural calling, which she obeyed, roaming ever deeper into the forest.

Mr Mickievič was convinced that his wife was ill. He kept asking about the state of her health, told her to see a doctor, going as far as to suggest that he would pay for a spa, but she just shook her head absently, insisting she was absolutely fine. The Mickievičes' flat no longer resembled the Mickievičes' flat. Forgotten objects pulled faces at Mr Mickievič wherever he went, the dust that was never swept away triggered his coughing fits and in the once practical household all sorts of useless things started turning up, such as stones, bird feathers or strange cavernous fruits. It was as if the rain forest were pushing its way out of the bathroom and trying to devour the entire flat, to grow all over it, spreading its roots and eventually ingesting it completely. Mrs Mickievič was no longer Mrs Mickievič, she was now Ágnes who roamed the rain forest and even though in the daytime her body went through the motions required to run the household and respond to Mr Mickievič's usual questions, there was a silent film running in her eyes as if the rain forest were growing directly out of her head.

And so Ágnes' soul kept peeling off night after night. Little by little, more and more each time, leaving in her bed just her mortal frame, which no longer resembled a woman's body but looked more like a greasy brown spot. The greasy spot dwindled steadily away until one night, when a full moon danced its wild dance above the city, all that was left lying next to Mr Mickievič was a tiny dark dot. Ágnes' soul roamed the rainforest as usual. The mysterious being whose presence she had long felt started to sing. A plaintive chant rose from the rotting trees on the ground. It whirled in the air, drowning out the screeching of the guerezas until it sank into the most sensitive part of Ágnes' soul. She sniffed the air like a dog, or rather she pricked up her ears and started running, as light as smoke, towards the source of the singing. There, on a huge boulder, glistening like a whale's tail, sat an old woman with the face of Ágnes' long-deceased aunt. The aunt that had been locked up in the asylum because she had heard voices inside her head. Her eyes burning, she clutched white skulls of humans as she drummed out the rhythm of her song. Ágnes recognised the song. Her memory conjured up the picture of a young woman on a summer night, singing a small child to sleep with a song about a naughty girl who got lost in the dark. The old woman smiled as if she could see the picture emblazoned on Ágnes' white soul. Her eyes blazed. Ágnes sat down beside her. She picked up the bleached skulls, started to bang them against each other, and a song burst from her throat. Just as the two women started to sing the second stanza and Mr Mickievič contentedly rolled over in bed, and as the moon's orange glow flooded the empty hallway, the bathroom door silently closed forever.

Julia

The evening takes the faintly lit room in its lazy embrace. Julia has just finished washing her body under the shower. It seems even paler than usual against the backdrop of brightly coloured towels hanging in the bathroom. She rubs in some aromatic oil and looks at her face in the mirror, lost in thought. The sound of an engine starting can be heard through the open window. He is waiting in bed. Julia is rubbing the oil into her dry skin. Slowly. Her skin greedily devours the greasy drops of oil. It is white. Like a china bowl, Julia thinks. He is lying in bed. Waiting. The sound of the car fades away. Julia lingers in the bathroom longer than necessary. She takes too long to comb the wet black hair that falls onto her shoulders. The hair feels cool. It sticks to her skin as if wanting to kiss her. With a pensive look she pulls the comb rhythmically, untangling the hair that got tousled as she washed it. The comb makes a sound. A rustling, whistling sound. He is waiting. Lying in bed. Julia hopes he will fall asleep. She is applying anti-wrinkle cream to her face. Against the past. Against time. Against the inevitability of aging. Very slowly. She hopes he will fall asleep.

Julia, he calls out. Why are you taking so long? She gives a start. She puts the comb down and twists her hair into a huge knot. I've knotted my head, it flashes through her mind as she turns off the bathroom light. She is naked. The tiny pubic hairs between her legs are breathing cleanliness. Her bare feet pitter-patter on the cool lino. She crosses the room lit by a single small light in one corner. Her white body floats above the rug. She looks like a ghost. I'm coming, she says.

I did promise, she tells herself. They haven't made love for three months but to her it seems like an eternity since they last did. Have they, in fact, ever made love? Slowly she approaches the bed, cautiously placing her feet on the rug like an animal nearing a trap. He is naked, too. Julia studies his big dark body, the chest hair, the curved toenails and the scar on his knee. She doesn't look at his face. Julia, he says, reaching out his hand to her. She hesitates. Standing by the bed she examines the little cushions of his palm. They are white. Like her body. As if her body had painted his hands. I did promise, she thinks, and the thought forces her to sit down on the edge of the bed.

His breathing is heavy. Julia feels his glance touch her back, move along her spine and stop at her bottom. You are beautiful, he says. She examines her white arms casually. It's been a while since we made love. An eternity, Julia thinks. He leans towards her. Slowly. Julia feels as if a shadow were approaching her. A large bird of prey. She starts to shiver and her alabaster skin comes out in goosepimples. You're freezing, he says and Julia can tell from his voice that he is turned on. He is right by her side. Shivers run down her spine. He sniffs Julia's back, taking his time. She feels his nostrils inhaling her like some enormous vacuum cleaner, siphoning off bits of her skin and the scent of soap. She feels as if he's going to snuff her out. She is still sitting on the edge of the bed. He cups her breasts in his hands. Impatiently. He squeezes them with his huge hands. As if he were squeezing out a lemon, she thinks. Her breasts look helpless in his hands. Taken aback. They don't know what expression to make. Julia looks at his face. It is filled with excitement, it's burning with excitement. Like a pot of milk that has boiled over. She has promised him. Paralysis grips her for a second. An animal caught in a trap.

He lays her on the bed gently. She feels as if she were falling off a cliff. She's trying to save herself. To find something firm to hold on to. There's something I've got to tell you, she says hurriedly. Something I saw today when I went shopping, Julia whispers. An animal trying to escape from the trap. Later, he whispers back, and Julia can feel the first kisses showering her belly. They are hot. Like boiling oil. They run, creating a thick film over her body. A film that prevents her from feeling anything. What I saw   says Julia. Later, later, he says, covering her mouth with one hand and spreading her legs apart. She doesn't feel anything. She can only hear. Hear his grunting, smacking, savouring. Greedily, getting his fill of her taste. Of the void inside her. Julia tilts her head back. Her eyes check the books on the bookshelf. All meticulously sorted. They are covered in dust. When I went shopping I saw... Julia whispers.

He doesn't hear. Deliriously he is groping the thin skin of her pink genitals. He's trying to penetrate her crotch, set it on fire. Burn through it. She rasps. Does it feel good? he asks but Julia doesn't reply. I did promise, she tells herself.

Julia doesn't feel anything. She is looking. At the books. The dust. She lets him turn her body around, lets him do as he pleases. She did promise. She lets him penetrate her. Images flash through her head. Such as the painting she saw on the wall of a ground floor flat. On her way to the shops. A curtain on the window moved aside for a moment and she saw the painting as she walked past with her shopping bag. The picture showed a large red eyeball in a glass. She didn't have time to look at it. Not properly. The painting was covered by the curtain. Now it has surfaced in her memory. She has plenty of time to examine every detail in her mind. The blood-red eye. The fine veins in the white of the eye. The eyelashes. The desperate way the eye was staring through the glass. She's got plenty of time. Meanwhile he's riding her body. Really hard. A wet cliff.

As her memory traces the infinitely black pupil of the eye, the sound emanating from his throat tells her that he has climaxed. The wet cliff has fallen off her. Julia, oh Julia, he gasps. He's lying next to her white body. Well, I did promise, didn't I, she thinks. Julia sits up, the image of the eye vanishes. She can no longer recall it. They are silent. He raises himself to light a cigarette. They are silent. The voice of a drunk coming home from the pub can be heard through the open window. He is smiling. With contempt, it seems to Julia. So what was it you saw on your way to the shops? he asks in a normal, unexcited male voice. Julia remains silent. She is trying to go back to the picture but her memory can no longer conjure up any part of it. Later, she says, it's not important now.

He flicks his ashes into an ashtray and says: We forgot to turn the light off. Somebody might have seen us. Julia shakes her head. The curtains hide everything, she says and goes to the kitchen to get herself a glass of water. Looking at her bare shoulders he draws on the cigarette. What is it, Julia? he says, pretending to try to understand her silence. Nothing, she replies and takes a sip of water. There is no eye in the glass. Nothing, she says again, just water. He sighs. A long, protracted sigh. The sigh sounds like the sea hitting a cliff. You're my wife, Julia, these things are normal, he says, trying to interrupt the silence. She says nothing. She watches the water in the glass. The surface of the water quivers along with her trembling fingers. She raises the glass and looks at it against the light. She spots his eye in it. It is brown. I know, says Julia and tips the remaining water into a plant pot. I know everything, she says.

They are silent again. He puts out his cigarette and starts reading a magazine. It has a big red car on the cover.

On the way to the shops I saw a picture in a window, she says. Hmm, he says, and keeps reading. But I guess it's not important, says Julia, casting a questioning look at her husband in bed. Hmm, he says, without raising his eyes from the magazine. Julia strokes her brow. Small beads of sweat stick to her hand. She pauses in surprise. What is it? he says, giving Julia a bored look. Nothing, she replies. Nothing, that's the point, says Julia, wiping the dust off the books with her fingers. The voice of the drunk coming home from the pub can still be heard through the open window. Exhausted, Julia finishes dusting the books and wipes her hands on the white curtain.

The Night Circus

Eleonora is walking along the streets. It's night and the damp, white fog curdles into thick semolina around the lampposts. Eleonora walks slowly. She lets her legs carry her aimlessly down the streets illuminated by shop windows. She doesn't look in. She notes the bright splashes of neon light that hit the white pavement, producing bright puddles. Silence reigns everywhere. The wind howls through an iron structure builders have erected in front of a derelict house. Eleonora's face looks pensive in the blue light of a window she's just passed. She's in no hurry, even though the clock tower has struck two.

She's walking. She meets no one. The lights in the houses have been turned off, and the cats wailing among the scattered piles of rubbish are the only sign of life. Eleonora is not aware of her body, only the empty streets. She listens to the echo of her footfalls. It reminds her of the sound of ping pong balls bouncing off a wooden table. The echo has its own rhythm, regular and flowing, interrupted only by her heels striking the pavement. She finds it very soothing. At night she creates music that sounds like a gently murmuring river, unlike during the day. Eleonora is irritated by the noise people make as they walk down the street. The sound coming from beneath their shoes is chaotic, restless. It strikes her eardrums with a vengeance and makes her feel anxious. At times like these Eleonora can't hear herself. The echo of her steps is drowned out by the savage rhythm of walking people. It makes her feel like she doesn't exist. Like she's just a ghost. A fiction. She's losing her outlines; she's nothing but an indefinable, shapeless thing. That's why she can't stand crowded streets, teeming with haste and noise, and that's why she only goes walking at night.

She leaves the outskirts behind. The concrete pavement turns into a gravel path. It's as white as snow and leads to a vast park. It's dark all around. Blackness shields her vision like a patch covering a gouged-out eye. There's not a single light to be seen. There's just a blue flicker of Eleonora's watch when the hand passes the half hour. The night swells up like a dense bubble as she enters the hushed park. Her shoes sink into the moist gravel. Eleonora is aware of the road gnashing its teeth in anger. It would like to gnaw off the soles of her shoes. To punish her for disturbing it. At two thirty in the morning. She smiles and digs her heels deeper into the gravel. The path gnashes its teeth more loudly. Eleonora drags her feet as hard as she can. A plaintive song resounds through the park. The wind rocks the tree branches. They groan in pain, like someone dying. Eleonora feels no fear. Perhaps she ought to, if she cared about herself. If she loved herself just a little. But she feels nothing for herself. Only surprise when she glimpses her own reflection in the mirror. A kind of unease about not feeling any affection for this body given her by providence. As if she were in it by mistake, conscious of having to feed it and clean it; as if oiling some kind of a curious tiny mechanism she inhabits, an unwelcome Christmas gift. Sometimes she pinches herself to make sure her body hasn't disappeared. She's surprised to find warm, dry skin. You ought to love yourself more, people say. You ought to care about yourself.

But she's incapable of that, and all she cares about is the echo of her steps in the deserted streets. A fine drizzle has started to fall. The bushes in the park are turning even darker than before. She passes a thicket. The grass she walks on has covered her shoes in slime. She's almost reached the end of the park when she notices a tent lit up by a neon sign. CIRCUS. No name. The neon light is red. No other words, just Circus. Eleonora comes to a halt. The grass stops licking her shoes.

She can hear drops of rain falling on the heavy canvas. A plastic clown stands at the entrance to the circus. His face is white and his big red mouth grins mutely into the darkness. Eleonora goes closer. In place of eyes the clown has slits for coins. She hesitates. She wonders what to do. Eventually she extracts some change from her pocket. She drops it in one of the slots. The clown's eyes open at the clink of the coin, giving off a purple flicker, and the cloth over the entrance is drawn aside. Eleonora enters.

It's a peculiar circus. Quite unlike the ones her parents used to drag her to. In fact, it's just a colossal ring strewn with silvery sand. There's no orchestra. No audience. And the interior is illuminated by a single red light. The ring is empty, chains and ropes dangle above her head. Eleonora walks around. The sand evokes the presence of the sea. She takes off her shoes. She removes her coat. She buries her feet in the silvery shingle. She sighs with pleasure. A female voice comes out of the loudspeaker: Welcome to our night circus. Relax. Put away your coat and make yourself comfortable. All safety regulations will be observed. The following stunts are on offer tonight: Taming of a Wild Beast, Trapeze Jumping, Knife-Throwing, Fire-Eating.

The voice is calm; it pauses briefly before repeating the menu. Eleonora stops to think what she might like to see. After a while she makes her choice. Taming of a Wild Beast, she calls out. Music starts to play. It's not really music; it's more like distant drumming, coming ever closer and getting louder. The light in the ring turns green. Eleonora sits on the floor, expectantly. The sound of drumming fills the whole space. Two men emerge from behind the stage and instantly erect a metal cage around Eleonora. They place a high stool in the centre, the kind on which tame tigers usually sit. The men cast an indifferent glance at Eleonora and leave. The tom-toms keep drumming. The chair gleams. Eleonora is sitting in the cage all alone. She's feverish with excitement. She feels a vein throbbing somewhere around her navel. The little mechanism inside her is waking up.

Eleonora stares at the door in keen anticipation. She's waiting for a lithe tiger to be ushered into the cage. The idea of finding herself face to face with a wild beast makes her shiver. She's not frightened, just very curious about what might happen next.

The cage door opens. A woman enters the ring. She's wearing black boots, black underwear, a garter belt, and gloves up to her elbows, all made of leather. She's holding a whip and has a silver-studded dog collar around her neck. Her white skin is luminous. She looks Eleonora in the eye. Eleonora registers that the woman's face is rather attractive. And quite strange. Slender. Inhuman. She notices a wart at the end of her nose. The woman smiles. Her smile is malicious, revealing beautiful, healthy teeth. Eleonora is still sitting on the floor, waiting for the wild beast to enter. The rhythm of the drumming changes. The woman approaches, takes off Eleonora's wristwatch, and clamps a collar around her neck and cuffs on her hands and feet. The watch flies out of the cage in a long arc. Eleonora realises that there are chains attached to the collar and cuffs.

The woman cracks her whip, and drags Eleonora on her belly towards the stool. Up! She commands, pointing her whip at the stool. Eleonora gets it. This is a game. The beast is in the ring. She scrambles up. The tamer shows her approval by patting her gently on her rear. The two men bring some hoops into the cage. They're huge, yellow, arranged one behind the other on a stand to form a tunnel. A narrow metal bench runs down the middle. The sound of flutes joins the drums. The tamer brings out a lighter and sets the hoops on fire. The flames start to lick them, quivering in the air and casting dancing shadows onto the sand. Jump! The woman commands again. Eleonora climbs off the stool and approaches the flames. She feels the heat of the burning tongues of flame. She thinks that her eyelids are about to be incinerated. Jump! The woman repeats. Eleonora's curious little mechanism knows no fear. Dreamily, she gazes into the blazing tunnel. It's a game, flashes through her head. The tamer's getting impatient and whips Eleonora across her thighs. It smarts. She grabs the tamer's hand and sinks her teeth into it. You beast, the woman screams and yanks Eleonora's collar. The dancing flames are menacing and alluring at the same time as they dart to and fro. Eleonora slowly enters the burning tunnel. Heat envelops her. She crawls down the tunnel, scraping her knees along the metal bench. The heat is licking her body. She's aware of her shoulders, her shoulder blades, her back. The smouldering air penetrates her nose. She can smell scorched hair.

Eleonora is in no hurry. The mechanism inside her is not scared. She's fully conscious of her body passing through the flames. Of absorbing them. As if it were bathing in them. The metal bench is red hot. A million needles shoot into her hands. When she reaches the end of the tunnel, she stops. She watches the fabric of her blouse burn as if she were watching the ring from inside a furnace. The tamer calls out to her. Eleonora is in no rush. It's a game. She's waiting for the bench to become unbearably hot. The leather-clad woman calls out to her again. Eleonora is in no hurry. The heat assaults her body like a rabid dog. The woman grabs the chain attached to the collar and drags her out. She's cursing. Eleonora resists. The bench is scorching her skin. As if about to devour her hands, she thinks. For a brief moment she has a feeling that a flame of red is slithering down her throat. The tamer yanks the chain abruptly. Eleonora stumbles out of the furnace, falling down to the floor. The men put out the fire and carry the hoops out of the arena. She's lying in the sand on her belly. Sweat pours off her face. The collars and chains scald her, she's filled with fire, she feels like an ember that happens to have rolled out of the fireplace. Her guts, eyes, and mouth are red hot. She smiles serenely.

The woman in boots picks up a bucket. She throws several litres of cold water over her. Eleonora drinks greedily, and as the water hits her skin, there's a hissing sound. Instantly, her clothes stick to her body. They hug her calves and thighs tightly as if they have shrunk. The tamer prods her with the whip to make her get up. Eleonora bites the woman's leg. The taste of waterproofed leather fills her mouth. The woman cracks her whip. The game continues. Eleonora stands up. She smiles even though her knees are trembling. The two men pass the tamer some straps through the cage bars. They're reminiscent of the harnesses used to keep babies from jumping out of their buggies. The tamer straps Eleonora in and tightens the buckle. Eleonora can hardly breathe. Another wild roll of the drums comes from the speakers. The tamer looks at her with a disdainful smile. The wart on her nose glows ominously. She attaches the straps on Eleonora's torso, arms and legs to ropes suspended from the top of the tent. Then she pats Eleonora's face. Eleonora tries to bite the woman's hand but the tamer is faster. She pulls her hand away and shouts: Up!

Eleonora is slowly raised into the air. The tamer prods her belly with the handle of her whip. Eleonora laughs. She's hanging in the air like a flying stork, her legs and arms splayed out. She's getting further away from the ground. The rope is being pulled by the two strongmen, while the music speeds up. She's being pulled higher and higher, right to the top of the round roof. Eleonora feels no fear. As she looks down, the woman and the two men resemble black beetles. Suddenly there's a tug and she starts coming down gently, in free fall. She's aware of the tickling in her stomach and the pressure in her lungs. The ground is slowly approaching her face as she glides down with her arms spread like a crane. She laughs out loud. The men and the woman look her in the eye. They're silent, but they exchange signals when her head is about to touch the ground.

It's a game, Eleonora thinks, and realises that this time she's being pulled up much faster. She imagines she's a bird flying infinitely high. To sing a song to the sun. When she gets to the top, a sudden tug almost takes her breath away. Then she falls, quickly and steeply, and she knows she's turned into a meteorite tumbling headlong to the ground. The force of gravity squeezes her intestines right up into her throat. Involuntarily she emits an inhuman scream. I'm flying, she thinks. The sand in the ring approaches her face at breakneck speed. For a moment she's convinced her head will hit the ground at speed, that she will drill right down into the underworld, drill into the Earth. But the powerful pull of the men's muscles stops her a foot and a half above the ground. The smell of sand dances in her nostrils. She's laughing manically. More, she shouts. The men and the woman look in her eyes for a while. And then the fun begins. A deranged ride up and down in a superfast elevator. As if she were sitting in a speeding train, her guts are about to leap out of her throat, her cells mingle with one another mid-air. She no longer distinguishes top from bottom, she feels she's about to jump out of her skin, and her brain is gripped by an insane ecstasy. The mechanism is turning into a living, supple body. She screams. She laughs and squeals. The game continues. The ropes squeak, the chains rattle, and the men's arms keep catapulting her up and bringing her to a halt just above the ground, as if they had turned into the levers of a flying machine. Up. Down. Eleonora is somewhere else. She's forgotten herself; she's melting in the sound of the drums and in her own flying, pulsating body.

The belt on one of her arms comes undone. As she flies close to the ground the buckle snaps and her head and body crash into the hard bars of the cage. The impact knocks the wind out of her, she feels as if she is passing through the cage, as if her heart and lungs have been ripped out and are now knocking against her ribs from the inside. As if hard stones were falling inside her guts. Gigantic purple circles dance in front of her eyes. The sound of the drums turns into a wailing cacophony. Eleonora passes out.

The trailer is lit by a single naked bulb fastened above a sink. Eleonora is lying on a bed, covered by a blanket with pink flamingos on it. The two men are bent over her, applying cold compresses. The woman in leather boots is sitting at a table, her head propped on her chin, pensively chewing her lower lip. Eleonora opens her eyes. One of the men strokes her hair. You feel OK? She moves her head slowly. There's a black canvas in front of her eyes, her head's buzzing. I feel dark, she says, trying to look around the room she's lying in. You gave us a real fright, says the man sitting at her bedside. Eleonora begins to make out the men, a bed, strange cupboards and bookshelves, a bright tablecloth on the table, and garish photos pinned to the wall. She sits up. She notices a red dragon tattoo on the hand of the man pressing the compress onto her forehead. Eleonora points to the dragon and tries to ask something, but instead of words a bilious yellow liquid gushes from her mouth. She throws up. The woman at the table turns away in disgust. The light bulb flickers and crackles as if about to go out.

The room is plunged into darkness for a while. Shit, curses the woman at the table, but then the light comes back on. The man with the red dragon wipes down the floor and the bed. The rag squeaks as it slides up and down, soaking up Eleonora's vomit. The air smells foul. Eleonora becomes aware of the pain she feels all over her body and that she's wearing her blue watch again. It shows 4:30 a.m. I'd better go, she says and tries to get out of bed. The man with the tattoo stops her. Not yet, you might faint somewhere on the way, we'll make you some tea. She slumps back onto the bed. The woman in leather boots is still sitting at the table. Eleonora watches her. The malicious smile reappears on her face. You ruined the show, she says as the man puts the kettle on. Eleonora doesn't reply. She examines her wrist. The belt is gone, but her wrist is covered in purple bruises. You ruined my show, the woman at the table says again, much louder this time.

The other man, the one by Eleonora's bedside, chides her gently. Come now, Irina, it could've turned out a lot worse. Eleonora notices he has a shiny silver tooth in his mouth. The man with the dragon tattoo makes the tea. The light bulb crackles again. It threatens to go out. Damned electricity, says Irina and lays her head down on the table. For a moment they wait in silence. The light bulb comes back on again.

The man with the dragon tattoo hands Eleonora a steaming cup of tea. She picks it up clumsily, cautiously, so as not to burn her fingers. The man sitting by her bed takes it out of her hands. I'd better hold it for her, Alex, she's still weak. Alex sits down on a chair next to Eleonora. I could feel my body, she says suddenly. She feels her forehead, and finds a huge red bump. Oh, that was the damned buckle, Alex adds. She ruined my show, Irina says again in a huff, she was supposed to be frightened, beg us to stop, not shriek and ask for more and more.

Eleonora lowers her eyes. I could feel my body... Sure, Alex interrupts, it was the damned buckle. I could feel my body at last, repeats Eleonora, massaging her stiff neck with the palm of her hand. The man with a silver tooth hands her the cup of tea. She takes a sip. It tastes like black elderberry with honey. I told you, Yuri, we shouldn't open at night, says Alex, getting up to rinse the rag in the sink. The sound of water going down the drain punctuates the silence. Eleonora drinks her tea. She feels the warmth spreading through her stomach. The buzzing in her head gradually dies down. The watch on her wrist flashes blue. It's five o'clock. Irina's lying on the table, her glove-clad arms limp beside her body. All we get at night are perverts, she says slowly; there's nothing we can do except half kill them. She seems fine now, Alex says, looking at Eleonora's bruise with concern. It's not my fault, she says as she downs her tea. It's just that I... We know, you could feel your body, Yuri finishes her sentence, and then the damned buckle.

What a strange circus this is, Eleonora says, I've never seen one like it before. Well, you're quite strange yourself, Irina says mockingly, quite a nutcase, I thought I'd never get you out of that burning ring. Eleonora strokes her own cheek, the memories slowly come back. Oh yes, the ring of fire, I really did feel... Irina rolls her eyes with boredom. We won't open at night anymore, says Alex. Eleonora is still sitting on the bed holding an empty mug. She realises just how bruised and tired she feels, but her soul is completely at peace. I'd better go, she says, placing the mug on Yuri's knees. Alex tries to persuade her to stay, but she's dying for a breath of fresh air. She looks for her coat. Irina gets up from the table and hands it to her. The two women gaze into each other's eyes for a while. I ruined your show, Eleonora whispers. I know, it's not your fault, Irina says in a steely voice. It doesn't matter, Eleonora says and opens the door. All that matters is the echo of her footsteps in the middle of the empty streets. She touches Irina's glove gently and steps out of the trailer.

It's an October morning, just before 5:30, and clumps of fog lie scattered on the pavement. They are rumpled like napkins on a table after a spectacular drinking spree. A shiny gravel path snakes in front of Eleonora. It's not raining, the birds have overslept today, there's silence everywhere. She starts walking. The pebbles are gnashing their teeth again. When she reaches the end of the park, she looks back. Although the circus is enveloped in a milky fog, Eleonora sees the light go out in the trailer window. She keeps walking, and the teeth-gnashing path flows into a concrete pavement. The first pedestrians have invaded the wet city. The hurried steps are still tentative before they unleash chaos. She walks to a bus stop to get away from it. She sits down on a bench in a transparent glass booth. The morning fog slowly begins to lift. Eleonora smiles. It's 5:30, and the first bus is due in ten minutes.

An Average Dead Father

It's been ages since I last saw him. The last image of his face snapped by my mind's camera is one captured by the eyes of a ten-year-old. A pallid girl with skinny arms and legs, terrified of his violent temper. Now he's lying in a coffin. In his black jacket and white shirt he looks like a distinguished intellectual. Not like the drunkard that he was. The funeral guests are silent. The smell of frankincense wafts around the room. This is my dead father. Father. For years my surname was the only thing that reminded me of this word. The plain fact that my conception resulted from a coupling that required his presence. I look at his face, now at peace. It shows no emotion. Like a bleak, cold sheet of ice on a window. His face never looked this peaceful. And even if it had, I have never seen it like this. All I ever saw was resentment. Anger.

I haven't seen him for ages. Because he had abandoned me. Denied me. Rejected me as soon as he and my mother were divorced. Now that I think of it he had ditched me a long time before that. Before I was even born. At the very moment of spurting his semen into my mother's womb to fertilise an egg, the moment he reached orgasm. That's when he abandoned me. He had never given a shit about me. Back then he must already have thought of me as just this weird, bothersome burden that had to be looked after and for whom he had to keep quiet at night. A screaming little kitten. He should have drowned me. I don't know why he made me. Well, I suppose this was a question he had never asked himself. Because if he had, he would have felt some urge, some obligation to go and see his daughter. Once a year, at least. To check how she was. But he had never asked himself that question and that's why we haven't met until now, on the last leg of his journey. His last journey.

Nobody is crying. Probably because nobody loved him. And even if anyone had, they would not be crying because one doesn't cry for a bastard like him. I'm not crying either. Why should I? I'm standing stiffly, hoping to ease my sense of alienation by reminding myself that this is my father. "He's your father, for God's sake," people used to say when I was little. "Why don't you go and see him?" But how can you go and see someone who has denied you, who has erased you, for whom you are just air, a nothing. Without air he would have died but without me he managed quite well. I couldn't bring myself to go and see him. The two images lodged in my head were at odds with each other. The first one captured father's drunken, furious face. The other showed father's back, lovingly bent over a puddle, trying to catch young frogs for me. He got mosquito bites while doing it. I could never decide which of the two pictures to believe. Which was my real father? Sometimes it seemed to me that both of them lied. Ever since I was little I hated boys who killed frogs. It felt like they were killing the image. Of his back. Of mosquito bites.

And so I never went to see him. Because he had never explained the thing about the two photos, and also because he had never told me that he didn't give a shit about me. He just didn't. If he had told me, he would have had to look me in the eye. So he made things easier for himself. Not for me.

His hands are folded across his chest, clutching gleaming rosaries. They had never held a rosary. I'm sure of that. His hands look unnatural. Even in death they can't get used to piousness. It occurred to me that this was my first opportunity to take a good look. A detailed look. At my father, not the rosaries. So I look at him and try to understand why all the demons I have ever seen in my dreams bore his face. In fact, he doesn't look all that frightening. An average corpse.

An average dead father. He can no longer hurt anyone. Or beat up anyone. Or shout at anyone. All he can do now is lie there waiting to be buried.

The priest has started to celebrate mass. He talks of God and forgiveness. Who will forgive me for never going to see him? Not even when he was in deep shit. Sick from the drink. When he became homeless. Maybe in the coffin. The Lord forgives us only when we're in the coffin.

Just as well he's dead. He has liberated me. From feeling that I have a father somewhere, that I should go and see him. And he, too, has been liberated. We were chained to one another. Somewhere deep down the thought of his daughter must have nagged at him. Even though he had left her in the lurch, intentionally and consciously, deep down, in his heart of hearts he must have felt oppressed by the sense of duty. The duty to go and see his daughter. Maybe he tried to drown it in drink, booze it out, burn it out of his system. Nonsense. You can never drown duty in drink. It weighs down on you. I know. Every time I saw demons in my dreams Duty would sit by my bedside in the morning. She would say, sternly, "He's your father, for God's sake." She would wag her finger. And I was scared. Scared that I would obey in the end and ring his doorbell. That he would open the door. The demon. My father. That he would say something. Something nasty. Something that would kill me. I was so scared that I couldn't leave the house.

The eulogy is coming to an end. I try to catch a last glimpse of the shape of my father's lips, thin like a proper clarinet player's lips should be. They are thin, and now they are white, too. "You have the lips of your father. You walk like your father. Your hair is like your father's, too," I kept hearing. I hated everything about me that resembled my father. I would look in the mirror wishing I could cut out these disgusting thin lips of his. Pluck out my hair and cut off my legs. I hated myself for looking like my father. And whenever my sister and

I got into a fight, the most humiliating thing we could think of saying was, "You're like dad." A slap in the face. It hurt, like being struck with a smelly wet rag.

But none of this matters anymore. Because he is dead. A dead father, that sounds much more noble. Much better than a drunkard, an alcoholic, a brawler. When people ask me about my dad, I will be able to say proudly, "He's dead." He won't be able to do anything, spoil anything. But he won't make anything better either. He's just gone. And I'm left here. His lookalike. His forgotten orgasm. I can invent stories of how great he was, how he used to play with me, that he was a brilliant clarinet player. I can turn him into a different father, one who never drank, the one from the frog image.

The lid has come down on the coffin and the black procession follows the hearse. Our feet squelch in the mud. Father lies in the coffin. He is quiet. He could never keep quiet. He could only yell. Smash glasses. Now he's as quiet as… the grave. A pheasant crosses the road. A brown potato. It runs for its life. Don't worry. He's dead, that father of mine.

The coffin is unloaded, ropes bite into the wood. It's time to put an end to it. To say something. Something that weighs down on me as a duty. Something I have never been able to say. Leaves fall from the trees in slow motion, like rain in a silent film. Say something. OK. As you wish. I open my mouth. I'm a mute magpie. And as the coffin scrapes the bottom of the grave, the words tumble out of my mouth: I forgive you, you… bastard. You… Father, you.

Three Women

The room was cold and inhospitable. The hospital bed linen was tinged with grey, the washbasin smelled of bleach, and the remnants of a colourless liquid shimmered at the bottom of the drip suspended from a stand. The lino on the floor reflected slivers of the setting sun. The hum of the air conditioning and the voices of nurses laughing rang in one's ears. Somewhere on the ground floor the cooks banged huge pots. Three women sat in silence by the dying woman's bedside, quietly telling their beads.

The dying woman was breathing heavily. An eternity seemed to pass between each breath in and out. One of the three women, the one with dyed hair, sighed loudly. "She's in pain, isn't she?"

"The doctor gave her a painkiller," the second, younger woman said, blowing her nose. "He wanted to put her back on the drip but I told him not to prolong her suffering." The third woman, tall and bespectacled, touched the dying woman's hand affectionately. She regained consciousness and her empty mouth, toothless like a newborn baby's, tried to say something to the three women. The tall woman bent down closer to her. "We can't hear you, Mummy, what is it you're trying to say?" The dying woman made an effort but managed to emit only an inarticulate, rough noise that sounded like the crying of young crows about to leave their nest for the first time. "Look, she's gesturing," the youngest of the women said.

All three women leaned over the bed trying to work out what the dying woman was saying. They tried to read her lips and studied her facial expression, hoping to decipher the frantic messages written on their dying mother's face. "Death robs us of speech so that we can't give away the secret of what's on the other side," said the blonde woman, breaking down in tears. "Don't cry, you'll make it harder for her to die," the others reprimanded her. A plaintive guttural noise, like the bubbling of boiling water, could be heard in the room while the woman's arms, which until now had lain lifeless by her side, started to flail about in front of their faces.

"She's pointing to her legs," the woman with glasses guessed. "Mum, do your legs hurt?" The dying woman nodded. "Give me a hand, let's put a pillow down there," the woman whispered. Slowly lifting the withered, broken body, they gently pushed a white pillow under her bottom. "Is that better?" the blonde woman asked. Their dying mother nodded, and a smile flashed across her wrinkled face. The women returned to their seats and said another Hail Mary.

"When do you think she'll die?" the youngest woman began. "She's a fighter, I bet she'll last till morning," the woman with glasses said, stroking her mother. "I don't mind staying till the morning, I don't want her to die alone," the blonde woman said through her tears. "Neither do I," said the youngest woman, and suddenly all three women were saying, "Yes, me too, we'll all stay here with her to the end, right to the very end."

Mother was out of it again. She smiled and her eyes wandered around the room. "God knows what she can see," the woman with glasses said, bending down again. "I've heard that the dead come to collect the dying. The people we used to know, people we loved. Do you think Auntie Mariska has come to get her?" They all looked around the room, looking for some sign of Auntie Mariska, but couldn't see anything apart from the shiny white paint on the wall. "Come to think of it, she's had a bloody hard life," the youngest chipped in. They all nodded. "A crazy dad, a sick mum, six children and a difficult husband," the woman with glasses added. "Oh God, it sure was difficult, wasn't it?" the blonde carried on and planted a kiss on her mother's cheek. "She deserves an easy death," the youngest one couldn't resist saying. All three nodded again.

"Do you think she's ever had an orgasm?" the woman with glasses asked, looking up. "I doubt it," the youngest said, "our dad didn't care two hoots about her, he used to come home from his weekly shift and stay just long enough to knock her up before he went back to work." They sat down by her bedside, concerned that she might never have experienced an orgasm. They watched her face. The blonde silently smoothed down her blanket.

"Do you think she's ever masturbated?" the youngest kept nagging. "Don't be silly, when would she have done that, she never stopped working, she was lucky if she got a good night's sleep," the woman with glasses said, slightly irritated. They were silent for a while. The dusk in the room thickened and expanded, the air vibrated, charged with electricity, and it felt as if the dark micro-particles of dusk that started floating about the darkening room passed right through their dying mother, taking her apart inside and carrying her away. They looked at her, fully aware that this was the last time. Their eyes traced the wrinkles, the birthmarks and liver spots on her skin, trying to commit her to memory so that they could recall her later, one day when they would wake up in the morning and she would be long gone to some place where neither a face nor a body was necessary. To retain an imprint of her presence and use it to gather the strength they would badly need on their own journeys. Journeys they would now have to make without their mother.

The dying woman was now breathing with ever greater difficulty. Her lungs undulated, hissing like burst balloons. She could no longer draw a full breath, as if air were escaping uncontrollably through holes that death had drilled into her lungs. They seemed to be about to give up for good.

"It reminds me of labour," the blonde whispered, "it's like contractions, like something is trying to push her out of her own body.

And her skin is like a baby's, have you noticed? All her wrinkles have smoothed out." The women took another good look at their mother's face and nodded their agreement. Death is a bit like labour inside out, the youngest philosophised. "Going in reverse, whoosh." She gestured with her arms, imitating a reversing car. "You just go back to where you came from. Actually, it's not all that terrible. And probably just as painful." The three women said nothing, picturing a woman in labour. The blonde took the dying woman's hand. It was blue. "She's going," she said and her voice in the air-conditioned room suddenly sounded like paper being ripped up.

The dying woman's breathing was becoming increasingly ragged. She was trying to tell them something but the women couldn't understand her. "Yes, Mummy," they said, "it's time to go, you can go in peace now, you've done everything you were destined to do. Everything is all right. We're here with you."

They stroked her hand patiently. But Mummy wouldn't die. Just when it seemed that she was about to breathe her last, that death was set to place the cover of eternity over her face, her lungs would suddenly draw in another blast of air. "Didn't I tell you, she's a fighter," the woman with glasses said. "She'll last till morning." Mummy's breathing got calmer. She was smiling. Maybe she could see the invisible Aunt Mariska or those gardens with flowers that she used to love. The women tried to imagine what she was going through. "Perhaps she's now met that stranger, the man who used to leave a rose on her doorstep every morning for a whole year during the war." They started to share their memories of Mummy. They wondered why she broke Dad's finger, recalled the time she smeared the toilet paper with chilli peppers. How she gave a neighbour such a fright in the cellar that the neighbour got her dead drunk. Each of the three women tried to recall the funniest story, the most incredible moment in her life.

As they immersed themselves in images of the past, which not even almighty death could ever take away from them, they began to smile.

They brought out biscuits and coffee because it was going to be a long night. They grumbled that smoking wasn't allowed and quietly watched the nurse take Mummy's blood pressure. "Her blood pressure is very low," the nurse said in the same tone that shop assistants use to announce that they have sold out of bananas. "It won't be long now, unfortunately." Tears welled up in the women's eyes, their faces contorted by crying, but then they remembered that they had come here to help their mummy die in peace. "What do you mean, 'unfortunately'?" they said. "She is ready to go but she's a fighter, she won't give in to death just like that, never in her life did she get anything for free."

The nurse left and the women sank into silence again. Dusk enveloped their bodies, reaching the hospital bed, but they didn't put the light on, to make sure it didn't disturb their dying mummy. "Let us pray," proposed the woman with glasses. "Maybe it will help her." And so they prayed, Hail Mary and Our Father, and prayers for the dead, while their mummy slowly passed away, breathing more and more slowly and heavily.

At times they thought she had died already but then her lungs would draw in more oxygen. "Mummy, you should go now," the youngest said, kissing her on the cheek. "What's keeping you here? Your work here is done." The blonde and the woman with glasses joined in, leaning over the bed and recounting everything their mummy had done, promising they would take care of her remains and give her a decent funeral, telling her what clothes they would put on her, and that they would look after her sister who would now be left alone, she should just go now, for goodness' sake. "From now on I'm all in favour of euthanasia," the youngest one said. "Nobody should have to suffer like this."

Mummy's breathing slowed down. Sometimes as much as five minutes passed between her inhaling and exhaling. Her face smoothed out completely. The calm she now emanated brought the youngest woman to tears. Look how beautiful she is... The old woman's chest sank for the last time, quietly, without hissing, like when you drop a scarf on the floor.

"I think she's gone," the woman with glasses said, holding a little mirror to her mother's mouth. The lungs had stopped for good. The mirror was clear. "People say that the dead can hear for several hours after they've died," the blonde whispered. The three women got up and bowed in the direction of the dead woman. They bowed deep, bending almost to the floor. They told her how much they loved her, and that she would be in their hearts forever. They touched her calm face. Nobody cried. The woman with glasses launched into her favourite song, by Hana Hegerová. The lyrics about ripening cherries and green branches, young boys and cakes from which the cherries have been plucked, sung in her trembling voice, travelled down the hospital corridor. The nurse pulled out the tube from the stiffened arms and expressed her condolences. The doctor confirmed the death. The youngest woman opened the window. Fresh air was sucked into the room, refreshing the women's tired brows. The women suddenly felt as if a burden had been lifted from their shoulders. Something heavy, sticky and cold, quite unbearable. Something painful, that they wanted to run away from and that was making them sob. But they didn't run away. They stood their ground. The blonde went to the washbasin and splashed some water over her face. She flicked the light switch. Light spread through the room, almost gouging their eyes out. The women pressed their eyelids together in pain. They waited for their pupils to get accustomed to the piercing light. The youngest poured out what was left of the cold coffee. They drank. They didn't speak. They looked at their mummy.

The woman with glasses stroked her neck. "Come on," she said in a thick voice, "we have to put her dentures back. Before she goes completely stiff." All three of them touched her motionless body almost at the same time.

Travesty Show

The sound of church bells tolled in the air, relentlessly forcing itself through the closed window. It seemed to tread on her eardrums, bouncing up and down, until she was forced to open her eyes. It was late afternoon. Morning still seemed trapped in the room, filled with dried flowers, glittery gowns and photographs stuck into the frame of a large mirror. Jelena scrambled out of bed. Last night´s performance had exhausted her. Feeling robbed of ten years of her life, she wondered what kind of mask she should apply to her face today to restore it to its original shape.

Jelena Horáčková never got out of bed before noon. Her lifestyle extended the nights and consumed early mornings. It had been at least thirty years since she last saw the sun rise, heard the dawn chorus or registered the rumbling of the rubbish lorry.

She put on her slippers with white bobbles resembling a bunny's tail. She made herself a cup of coffee. Mechanically she sank into a huge, slightly tacky armchair, sweetened her coffee and stared ahead. Jelena Horáčková was once a megastar. Her concerts used to sell out, photos of her face adorned every magazine cover and hordes of fans used to write her love letters. Jelena's distinctive voice could be heard on every radio station and people bought her records by the dozen. She starred in every gala and New Year show. She was the heart and soul of the music business, an icon wooed, pampered and hated in equal measure. She once believed that things would stay like this forever, that her star would never stop rising, and that she would eventually become immortal. However, over the past ten years, the damned ten years as she used to say, she came to realise that offers of TV shows had dwindled, that she appeared in one concert a year at most, and the letters from lovesick admirers seemed to have dried up. At first she regarded this as just a passing phase, Lady Luck having turned aside for a moment, a mistake that would soon be put right, but then, one morning, as she stood in front of the mirror without her make-up, in her tired robe and with swollen eye-lids, she realised she was getting old.

She had never given any thought to old age. And why should she have done? In an industry that trades in beauty, talent and performance, nobody ever talks about age. People had been telling her for so long that she was gorgeous and brilliant and that she looked fantastic, that she got used to it and took all the praise for granted. Except that the praise and the invitations began to grow scarce and when her agent informed her that he was done with her because nobody gave a toss about an old fossil singing schmaltzy songs about love, it was as if her entire world had fallen in. It wasn't just a question of money. Jelena was aware that singing and dancing was the only thing she could do. She realised that it was too late for her to learn to do anything else and that her bank account was emptying rapidly. But what hurt more than anything else was the thought that she would end up old and on her own, in some dreadful hole.

Jelena was sentimental. All her life she had waited for the love of her life, someone she would meet in the changing room after a concert, who would hug her and protect her, her Prince Charming arriving in a white Rolls-Royce, quick-witted, gentle and, of course, fabulously rich. And since she was endowed with a magnificent imagination, she came to believe in this fantasy and never noticed that the men she met in her changing room were not princes but scroungers who took advantage of her as soon as she spread her legs, who would let her take them out and keep them and then ran away when it looked like they had to commit. And so Jelena staggered from one unhappy love affair to the next, convinced every time that this was it, the real thing. But it never was.

And that is why she was now sitting alone in her large tacky armchair with a cup of coffee sweetened with artificial sweetener to make sure she didn't put on weight, staring into the air. Her place was a mess, just like her life. And since she had never been a fighter, she just withdrew and spent her days weeping, occasionally performing at private functions organised by ageing sentimental pseudo-businessmen. Some people tried to convince her to have plastic surgery and a general makeover but the thought of a surgeon's scalpel cutting into her flesh made her stomach turn. For she knew that if the surgeon messed up, she would end up looking even worse, with twitching eye-lids, frozen lips, and her face would eventually disintegrate. She no longer had to rush anywhere or put on makeup when she took out the rubbish, journalists paid no attention to her and occasionally, but only occasionally, a former fan would recognise her in the street. She could now wear shapeless, dowdy clothes, and increasingly did just that. She no longer had to wear heels that tormented her feet, she could throw out waist-cinchers or shaping tights and, most importantly, she could stop dieting. And so she got up and went to the kitchen to fix herself a hearty breakfast. Bacon and eggs, bread and jam, sweet hot chocolate and a bowl of ice cream to top it all. In her heyday she would have felt guilty for at least a month if she had this kind of breakfast and she'd have spent another month sweating it off in the gym. Jelena stuffed herself greedily, flipping through the post that had been sitting on the table for a week. She smacked her lips. The gas and electricity bill robbed her of her appetite for a moment but then she forgot about it and treated herself to another portion of ice cream.

There wasn't a single invitation to a gig in the post, not a single contact worth mentioning. Just a bank statement, some junk mail and a letter in a white envelope. She looked at the sender's address and since it didn't ring any bells she decided it must have come from a former fan, one who'd probably had a lobotomy and failed to notice that her star had faded once and for all. She opened the letter. Her greasy fingers left an unappetising stain on the paper. It was an invitation, printed in golden letters on pink paper, to their forty-year high school reunion. She was taken aback. It had been a long time since anyone had invited her to anything. She reread the golden script and pictured her old school, the classroom and the caretaker who constantly berated them. In her mind's eye she saw her classmates, boys and girls; a blurry vision, like opaque glass in a door. She tried to recall their faces, names and characters. She couldn't remember a single person.

The date on the invitation stated that the reunion was today at six p.m. at the Lion Restaurant, a second-rate establishment whose menu boasted cheap wine and faux fillet steak. She hesitated. She wasn't sure if she dared to face up to her own youth, if she felt like going back forty years and dredging up memories that suddenly seemed beautiful, if painful. She paced around her flat for a while. Lost in thought, she kicked away a pair of tights lying on the floor. She went through all the pros and cons, even started to write them down in a list, like a psychologist had once recommended. The cons column included mostly words relating to her appearance, financial situation, her painful decline. The pro column brimmed with curiosity, loneliness and boredom, new contacts and the long awaited Prince Charming. By the time she made up her mind the clock showed quarter to three. She cleared the table, chasing away the flies that started to stretch their legs on it. She went to get ready.

This was Jelena's area of expertise. At the height of her fame she would sometimes take as long as four hours getting ready. She ran a bath, threw in some fragrant herbs and applied a nourishing mask to her face. It was the colour of mildewed spinach. She submerged her body in the water. Water calmed her, buoying her fat belly, lifting it up. She exhaled with pleasure and burst into one of her old schmaltzy love songs. Of course. All of Jelena's songs were about love. Or about parting. She sang and sang, the dripping tap merging with her singing to create a rhythm of its own. Her spirits improved considerably, she felt she had made the right decision and actually began looking forward to the event. Her memory conjured up fragments of faces and half-forgotten names of classmates she hadn't thought of for years. Zdeno, her mouth suddenly uttered. Yes, Zdeno, her classmate once caught by a teacher as he tried to seduce a girl from their class in the gym changing room. The memory of Zdeno improved her mood even further.

Jelena rubbed herself dry with a towel and washed off the remains of the nourishing mask. She opened the wardrobe and examined every item in her splendid collection. She took out the gowns she had once performed in, the red one with glittering sequins, the shocking pink one with stripes along the sides, the flowing long skirts and flowery blouses, belts, hats and fine gloves, rummaging through everything and unable to decide. In the end she picked a rather plain dark blue dress discreetly covering her wilting shoulders. As she opened her robe she noticed her sagging breasts in the mirror. *Pious breasts* flashed through her mind, but that idea spoiled her mood instantly so she quickly squeezed them into a push-up bra. She applied sober makeup to her wrinkled face and refrained from using lipstick, something she had never done before. She put on a hat, slipped a wallet into her handbag and slammed the door shut behind her.

Everyone had already arrived. Men in boring grey suits, women in shapeless dresses of an uncertain colour. They all merged into a grey mass of bald, ageing, potbellied men, and women reeking of cheap perfume. "Jelena," exclaimed an old man, rushing to meet her. "We didn't think you'd come," said a woman with freshly permed hair. Jelena had a vague recollection that she used to wear a brace on her teeth.

"Oh, but of course I had to come, how could I miss such a splendid occasion?"

The old man gave her a slobbery kiss. "Do you remember me?" he shouted, putting on an enthusiastic expression. Jelena stood still trying to remember who he might be but his face was an empty mirror to her. Without a past. "Ivan, I'm Ivan, remember I used to sit at the front, right by the door." Jelena pretended to remember who he was and where he used to sit, and flashed him a warm smile. "Oh yes, Ivan, of course…" she said politely and took a seat at the table.

They all kept glancing in her direction. Two women whose names and faces meant nothing to Jelena exchanged contemptuous smiles.

She felt uncomfortable. She was on edge, nailed to her chair by the silence and the glances. Ivan came to her rescue. "Let's drink a toast to our reunion after all these years," he said, raising his glass. The smell of cheap vermouth hit her nose. Ivan delivered a toast, something about this being just one of many occasions they would get together in great numbers and good health, hoping everyone would have a wonderful time, how happy he was to see everyone there and that he was pleased to be able to welcome their honoured guest, the singer and pop star who managed to carve out some time from her busy schedule to attend the reunion, the famous Jelena Horáčková. Someone sniggered. People downed their drinks. Food and wine arrived at the table. By now Jelena was regretting her decision to come. A fat man who sat across the table examined her inquisitively. She felt as if he were dissecting her breasts, touching her face, weighing up and comparing, and pearls of sweat appeared on her forehead. She wiped them off. Her makeup left a brown trace on the napkin. "I can't recall your name," she said, and a soup noodle fell out of her mouth. The fatso stirred in his chair and rapped out, "I'm Zdeno."

Jelena took a better look at him and indeed, she began to make out Zdeno's arrogant, smiling look. "Zdeno!" she smiled, this time not just to be polite. "I wouldn't have recognised you."

"It's the belly," he said, "I put on weight after I turned thirty and haven't been able to shake it off since." He grabbed his Michelin tyre and gave it a disgusting shake. Jelena was revolted but finished her soup. She had the second course as well and was too full for the dessert. "Thanks, I can't anymore," she said when her classmates offered her their home-made cakes. "Oh, I see, the pop star has to watch her weight," one of them taunted her. On hearing that, Jelena reached for the biggest piece of cake and stuffed it angrily into her mouth. Stupid cow, she thought, as she chewed away. She wondered who the woman in the appalling flowery dress might be. She stared at her face, examining her expression in minute detail. It wasn't until she reached the birthmark next to the ear that it all fell into place. Olina! Her best friend from school; they used to laugh that she had a light switch next to her ear. "Olina!" she yelled across the table. Olina burst out laughing. "About time you worked it out!"

Jelena moved over. "For heaven's sake, Olina, just look at us! Good job you've still got your light switch! I wouldn't have recognised you otherwise." Olina gave her a hug and she felt the familiar smell she used to breathe in when they changed after PE classes, the smell of slightly sweaty skin. Like hazelnut ice cream, flashed through Jelena's head.

"What on earth have you been up to, old girl?" Olina began. "You never came to any of our reunions so I thought, oh well, she's a celebrity, she doesn't give a toss about us plebs, but over the past few years you haven't been on TV very much either."

"You see, Oli, it's not my scene anymore, you know what it's like in show business, you're up one day, and down the next," said Jelena, pointing to the floor.

The conversation began to flow. People produced photos of their children and grandchildren, their houses and holidays, dogs and cats. Their weekend cottages and expensive leather sofas, their valuable art collections. Jelena listened to their stories and realised she wasn't so badly off. And, more importantly, she wasn't alone. She didn't take out of her handbag the photos of her gigs or those showing her with famous people. She didn't feel like answering awkward questions about husband and children, and explaining that all her Prince Charmings turned out to be scroungers. She didn't want to talk about the long, lonesome boozy nights. Or about the lonely changing rooms, the fleeting moments of happiness that follow the final curtain. She listened. She listened until midnight, until her classmates started to disappear. Zdeno was the only one in a party mood. "Come along, Jelena, don't be silly, who knows, we might be pushing up the daisies next time round," he joked. Jelena finished the wine that no longer seemed so awful and agreed to go along.

The establishment he dragged her to was full of bizarrely dressed, long-legged ladies in silver stockings and glittery knickers. They paid to go in. She was confused to hear the women speak in male voices. On the stage the MC was just announcing the next round of a contest. They took seats at a small table with a lamp that bathed them in a blue glow. "What sort of place is this?" Jelena wanted to know. "You'll see," he said with an enigmatic smile. "It's great fun, although the drinks are on the expensive side."

"And now, lay-deees and gentlemen, let me open our one and only contessssst for the besssst Jelena Horáčková, members of the jury, please return to your sssseatssss," the MC proclaimed. Fanfares sounded and shiny disco lights from the ceiling bathed the audience in a silver glow. A waiter asked what they would like to drink. Jelena ordered a glass of wine with a little water. She didn't want to get drunk. Six glittering Jelena Horáčkovás appeared on the stage, all wearing beautiful gowns, identical to those in her wardrobe. They wiggled their bums provocatively, wearing armbands and pearls in their hair, their faces perfectly made up. Jelena's jaw dropped. She thought she was in a dream. "I can't believe this," she stammered. The sound of her voice came from the playback. The first Jelena in a red gown, an exact replica of the one she could no longer squeeze into, picked up the microphone and started singing. The song 'Your Eyes Are Bluer Than the Sky', the hit of the 1965 season, dripped into the auditorium like treacle. The singer in the red dress wore an expression just like hers, puckered her lips just like she did and waved her arms, inviting the audience to clap. The fun began. Zdeno squealed with joy, triggering the first applause of approval. "What sort of place is this, Zdeno?" Jelena shouted, trying to make herself heard over the music. "Jelena, dear, welcome to the Travesty Show," he yelled into her ear.

Jelena sat back and drank as one Horáčková after another mounted the stage, all looking just like she had thirty years ago, singing her hits such as 'The Autumn of Passion' and 'I Still Love you', gyrating as they gave a perfect impression of her. She was watching herself. At times it seemed funny. But then again at others she felt like crying. "I knew I'd surprise you," said Zdeno, noticing a strange expression on Jelena's face. She sighed. "But you've got to admit that I was amazing," the real Horáčková said after a pause. She felt a twinge of envy. The audience was having a great time, people applauded and the older ones among them sang along with the fake Jelenas. She envied them the thrill, the aura of success, the floodlights and the dresses that made them look so slim. She felt as if she were watching a show of her youth, one she could never see because she had herself been on stage. It wasn't the same on TV. When it was the turn of a Horáčková who wore her favourite black dress with deep cleavage exposing a pair of wonderfully firm breasts, Jelena at the table grew sad. The song 'You'll Never Be Mine' reminded her of one of the Prince Scroungers, one she must have been really in love with.

She began to sniffle. When Zdeno got a whiff of her tears, he shot out of his chair and dashed towards the MC. He whispered something in his ear. The Horáčková in the black dress finished singing and the MC in a shiny blue suit shouted, "Lay-deees and gentlemen, tonight we have the great honour of welcoming the sssstar and ssssssinger

Jelena Horáčková in persssssson." The fanfares sounded again. Jelena was at a loss. She gave Zdeno an angry look and tried not to draw attention to herself. But the audience turned their heads trying to locate her and Zdeno pointed his finger straight at Jelena's head. A spotlight stabbed her in the eye. "Go on, get up there, go, go," said a flustered Zdeno, nudging her. "You shouldn't have done that," she said through gritted teeth. Jelena got up and as she negotiated the narrow path among chairs she thought that she wasn't dressed appropriately and properly made up and wondered why she had got herself into this.

A microphone was thrust into her hands. The MC said something to the musicians and her 1969 hit, 'Don't Leave Without Me', came from the speakers. Her voice trembled slightly but the familiar environment, the spotlights and the audience dispelled her fear and she felt like the person she used to be. She began to sing the sentimental song, which was, of course, about love, while the fake Jelenas undulated around her, the music played and the audience grinned broadly.

Once she calmed down she noticed that the audience included two Madonnas, a Diana Ross, an Amanda Lear, the whole of ABBA and three Suzi Quatros, as well as a few other pop stars she couldn't quite put a name to. She realised she had never sung to stars like these. Never mind that they were fake, she suddenly felt as if she had grown taller; her breasts perked up, her wrinkles disappeared and she turned again into the young and beautiful Jelena Horáčková, pop singer and star. Both fake Madonnas applauded, Diana Ross danced with Amanda Lear, and she sang her heart out as never before. Down in the auditorium Zdeno was shrieking at the top of his voice. When she finished, the roar of thunderous applause from the audience made her float a metre above the floor. She stroked the fake Jelena's red dress, admired the breasts of the Jelena in the black gown, complimented all of them on doing a brilliant impression of her and returned to her seat.

"Zdeno, I think I'm going to kill you," she said through her teeth while the jury announced the results. Jelena congratulated the winner. The party went on. She and Zdeno danced the night away. It was five in the morning by the time they left. Her feet were killing her. Trams were timidly cutting through the morning fog and she heard the first thrushes sing. She realised she was covered in sweat. The bags under her eyes ran down her cheeks. I must look awful, Jelena thought. But for the first time in her life she didn't care. She and Zdeno held hands and she noticed his white belly protruding from his open shirt, his matted hair and his trousers hanging low. She didn't feel repelled. For the first time in a long time. All she felt was an irresistible urge to invite him home for a cup of coffee.

Lace

The wart on her right cheek kept growing. At first, it was just a tiny black dot that Magdaléna noticed in the mirror as she washed her face. She didn't attach great importance to it. She had got used to the fact that her body was changing as it aged, so she was not thrown by the first age spots on her hands or the small brown warts on her neck. Magdaléna was a composer. Although she worked at a dry cleaner's, she composed the most wonderful melancholy piano preludes in her head. She could not play the piano. She could not read music and was unable to sing even the simplest nursery rhyme. She could only hear the music in her head. It played there every day with great urgency, filling her completely from within and dilating the pupils of her eyes. It resonated in her heart and pulsated through her blood vessels and every single muscle, sometimes making her entire body tremble as if she was gripped by fever.

At such moments, Magdaléna stopped stuffing clean clothes into transparent polythene bags and opened her mouth wide, to stop the music from tearing her body apart. Her colleagues taunted her, saying there she was going again, doing her carp-out-of-water impersonation; some of them even took pictures of her on their phones. Magdaléna wasn't deaf. She knew her mouth didn't emit any sound. It was a curse. The minute the music left her body, it evaporated. It simply disappeared without leaving a single acoustic trace of the perfection which sprang from within her head and for which she had no name. I'm missing a channel of communication, she thought.

She would never forget the day the music invaded her head. She was going to have lunch at a café across the road from the dry cleaner's. There was a wonderful smell of sautéed liver and the clanging of enormous pots. Magdaléna heard the loud clinking of cutlery being tossed into a metal tray. Suddenly the kitchen noises melded into a rhythmic tune, which intensified and was gradually joined by various musical instruments. Ever since then, Magdaléna had lived all by herself, immersed in her music. Her mornings were filled with brisk bagatelles and her evenings were full of depressing fugues. Extraordinary things happened during thunderstorms. Her head roared and her hair became electric, as if she were connected to a transformer station. A stormy symphony resounded inside her, wind and string instruments drowning each other out and the percussion booming so loudly that she sometimes fell into a trance. Any activity that produced a sound launched an avalanche of continuous melody, so that sometimes at work she was transported by the rustling of polythene or the hum of a flushing toilet.

She began to worry about the wart that appeared on her face. Not only was it growing but it started excreting a kind of fibre. Delicate capillaries stuck to her skin, creating a bizarre, flowery pattern. It's growing like English ivy, she thought one evening. She picked up a magnifying glass and thoroughly inspected the cobweb that had, by now, covered the lower part of her jaw. The capillaries linked up into intricate patterns, creating black lace that reminded her of magnolia blossoms. The lace was growing by the day. Magdaléna noticed that the music in her head was also growing in intensity and the sounds it contained were becoming ever stranger. The sounds of piano and strings were punctuated by weird electronic sounds and industrial rhythms, making her feel as if she was listening to a singing tin factory. It all started to get a bit tiresome. The rhythm was accelerating and she caught herself throwing dirty laundry into a white van at a frantic pace.

One morning, when a steel drum machine was roaring away in her head as she was whisking eggs, she decided she had to do something. She made an appointment with a dermatologist. In a mocking tone, the doctor asked about her mental state, but after she examined her through a magnifying glass she was dumbstruck. "Incredible," she said opening an enormous book and browsing through it for a while. "Perhaps it's a degenerative form of wart? Have you been sunning yourself a lot?" she enquired, but Magdaléna assured her that she had hated the sun ever since she was a little girl. The doctor continued leafing through the encyclopedia for a while, then said with a sigh, "Let's try Locacid."

Magdaléna applied the ointment to the wart every day. Yet it kept growing, covering all of her neck and half her face and spreading lower and lower still, as if it was trying to envelop her completely. The wart did not respond to anything. Ointments, liquid nitrogen, even laser treatment could not stop it from excreting more capillaries. Magdaléna was changing. Not only were her face, neck, arms, and torso now covered by a continuous layer of lace, but she started emitting music. Yes. The tunes she had managed to contain for years now began to rise to the surface, streaming out through the lace loudly, wildly. She turned into a music-playing, a kind of lacy larva, from which a strange butterfly might one day emerge. Crowds of people started coming to the dry cleaner's to gape at her and turnover went up by three hundred per cent. Nor was Magdaléna's body what it had been. The lace had extended into her muscles and she found she was much more pliable and could now bend into the shape of a bridge without the slightest effort.

"I'm convinced that you are a case well beyond the scope of science. We have to contact international experts. Whole symposia will be devoted to you!" the doctor said during a check up. At that moment Magdaléna was playing jazz and her body, completely covered in lace, was swaying to its rhythm. "Can you hear it?" Magdaléna asked. "Why do you need a scientific explanation, I've just relaxed, that's all." The doctor nodded resignedly. "Do you hear the music at night too?" she asked. Magdaléna explained that at night she played organic ambient music, which enabled her to get some sleep. "Except I don't feel like sleeping," she whispered. "I'm just bursting with energy. You know how many wonderful pieces I can compose this way? I thought I might start recording; I've even had an offer from a radio station." The doctor went on about the importance of sleep and tried to hand her a prescription for some medication, but a wave of furious break-beat washed over Magdaléna, sweeping her out of the doctor's office, out of the hospital, and into a distant park.

The music bursting out of her through the lace was getting heavier. Autumn was coming and Magdaléna noticed that in the morning she played increasingly hard rock spiked with elements of heavy metal, so she stopped taking the bus to work. Few people could stand being next to her. The music was too loud and customers at the dry cleaner's started complaining. "Why don't you take unpaid leave?" her boss suggested after Magdaléna came to work playing hardcore punk. "I'll try to tune into something gentler, like reggae," she tried to reassure her, but her boss just clutched her head, screaming, "Turn her off, somebody, for God's sake!"

Magdaléna began to avoid people. She sought out remote places in mountain parks with frightened squirrels as her only company. One evening, when the moon was full and she was again unable to sleep, a heart-rending jungle beat made her wander far beyond the city limits. In a meadow overgrown with brambles she stumbled upon some people dancing. They were lit by the headlights of parked cars and a girl with headphones was playing music on curious-looking turntables. Magdaléna smiled. Her spirit connected to the house music streaming from the speakers. The lace was burning, her skin was stretching, and her heart was pounding madly. After a few hours of dancing, Magdaléna's body burst. A huge white bat flew out. After noiselessly circling above the heads of the dancers a few times it disappeared into the quiet darkness that emanated from the depths of the forest.

Apricot

A yellow butterfly fluttered around the red ribbon buried in her grey hair. Taking the little bucket from my hands, Miss Priska emptied the coffee dregs onto the ground next to the tree. I watched the earth absorb the remnants of our morning Turkish coffee. The butterfly performed an elegant manoeuvre to taste the wet, coffee-flavoured soil. "I hope it won't give it a heart attack," I said but the old lady just waved it away, sending a stream of water from her hose onto the gnarled apricot tree. It must have been in our courtyard for at least a century. Miss Priska was seventy-four, with a gorgeous shock of silvery hair.

She lived alone in a first floor flat with a small garden, surrounded by an enormous brick wall. In spite of her seventy-four years she was out there every day tending her fringed Dutch tulips, purple irises and sugar-puff-like pink hydrangeas. "Coffee and Elvis, there's nothing better to give a girl a lift," she said, slowly walking over to her flat to turn up the record player. The tree's branches swayed in the draught generated by 'I Got a Woman'. Miss Priska was an Elvis Presley fan. An aged Elvis Presley fan, to be more precise. If it hadn't been for her wrinkled face and white hair I would have thought this was a crazed girl in a fifties polka-dot dress by Christian Dior. She listened to the King of Rock every day, humming to the flowers in her husky voice on long summer afternoons. Her flat was crammed with the most absurd assortment of trinkets bearing Elvis's likeness: sugar bowls, glasses, doilies, statuettes and plates; she even owned a toothbrush adorned with his portrait. That she never used. Displayed in a goblet behind glass it looked as if Elvis had only just finished brushing his teeth. "He's a kindred soul," she would say, knowingly caressing a wall hanging showing a life-sized Elvis, microphone in hand. "We might have met if it hadn't been for the Pond, but who would have wanted to cross the Atlantic?" she added with a gesture indicating she wasn't going soft in the head.

Miss Priska was the oldest resident in our block. The only thing possibly older than her was the fruit tree that she looked after so affectionately. She was lonely. Over the years she had lost her siblings and most of her friends had been pushing up the daisies for quite a while. She knew the history of every flat around the courtyard. She remembered ancient gossip and long-forgotten love triangles. "The only ones left are me and her," she said, gesturing towards the old tree with a chin that made her look like a storybook picture of an old witch. The apricot tree had borne no fruit for years. That didn't stop Miss Priska from tending to it with touching care. She would prune it, hoe around it, and treat it with fertiliser. She kept looking for new recipes guaranteed to give the tree a new lease of life so that she could taste its delicious fruit once again. "You wouldn't understand unless you'd tasted it. It's a rare variety. A Turkish pasha brought it straight from Istanbul as a gift for Miss Eržika. Eržika had lived on the third floor and the Turk fell madly in love with her after they met at a health resort. Now they're both long gone, you see? But the apricot tree is still here!"

Miss Priska looked after the tree throughout that strange summer, during which heat waves alternated with sudden downpours, making the grass grow faster than she could mow it. The garden turned into an exotic jungle, with shoulder-high grass and pink hydrangeas resembling street lamps lit in the middle of the day. That July morning I came to see Miss Priska with my usual offering of coffee dregs. I ran down the two flights of stairs barefoot, carrying a whole week's supply, which was beginning to ferment at the bottom of the little plastic bucket.

"I won't be needing the coffee anymore," Miss Priska announced, bursting with joy. Her voice was trembling with emotion. The sparks flying from her eyes nearly scorched my bare feet. She stood there pointing to the apricot tree, as if to introduce it or induct it into the Hall of Fame. "Time to start making preserves!" she exclaimed triumphantly and handed me a yellowish-red fruit. "Have a taste," she said, jabbing me as I glanced from my hand to the tree and back in astonishment. The tree was groaning under the weight of all the fruit on its branches. The ground around it was strewn with fallen fruit, which must have been pullulating with worms.

"I can't believe this," I gasped, biting into the soft apricot flesh. As I swallowed, my tongue was drenched with the sweet juice. "What does it taste like? Tell me!" Miss Priska shrieked euphorically.

"It tastes like, like… pineapple dusted with vanilla?" Flabbergasted, I struggled to find words to describe the unusual taste. "Bingo!" she shouted and walked briskly into her flat to put on her favourite record. Elvis's deep voice came bounding over the garden wall, the wailing guitar sending a cat scuttling away.

"'Blue Suede Shoes' always makes my blood race – here, go and get me twenty pounds of sugar," Priska ordered, pressing money into my hands. Before I left, the old lady began to dance: it was something vaguely resembling rock'n'roll.

For a whole month the smell of apricot jam kept prising open the windows of our block with its finger. It tweaked the noses of the sweet-toothed neighbours. They sat watching TV and salivated onto their carpets. Apricot jam, stewed apricots, apricot butter, dried apricots, apricot custard. I must have hauled tons of sugar from the shop and still the tree wouldn't stop bearing fruit. Every morning its branches were freshly laden, forcing Miss Priska to store the preserves in every available space, including the toilet. "Would you like some apricots?" she kept badgering her neighbours, who just shook their heads. The fruit fell to the ground, rotting and fermenting, but Miss Priska kept at her labours tirelessly.

"This is crazy," I said one evening, after making one of my regular deliveries of sugar. Priska dipped her hand into a baby bath full of squashed apricots and said with a devilish smile, "I've discovered a brilliant recipe for apricot shampoo, it's supposed to make one's hair grow like nothing on earth!"

I glanced at Priska's grey hair, twisted into a giant bun. "You should stop now or all this preserving will drive you completely round the bend."

She shook her head stubbornly. "Just look at the tree, my dear!" The apricot tree was still heavy with vast quantities of fruit. Every inch of it was covered in small, velvety, yellowish-red balls. By now the tree resembled an apricot tart melting in the sun. Huge amounts of sweet fruit lay rotting around it. Fat wasps circled the banquet, their fussy buzzing audible to everyone in the building. Miss Priska stopped sleeping. She started playing her Elvis rather more loudly than appropriate and continued to collect the fruit tirelessly. Every morning she found more fruit on the tree's branches.

The omnipresent sweetish smell irritated my stomach. I kept having to rush to the toilet and throw up. I noticed that where my hands had touched the apricots they had changed. The skin became tauter and more supple. They looked like smooth little baby hands, without any lines, hangnails or blotches. Miss Priska started to change, too. Her complexion became taut and smooth. The wrinkles vanished from her face, her grey hair was transformed into fresh black tresses and she looked years younger. With brisk steps she darted around the garden to the rhythm of the music, looking like a schoolgirl in her hideous polka-dot dress.

"I'm not buying you another ounce of sugar, Miss Priska!" I declared one day. "You've got to do something about that tree. Look at yourself, just see what you look like! It's really dangerous!" Priska gave a deranged giggle. "From now on, call me Priscilla," she snarled, sampling another batch of apricot jam bubbling on the stove. "I feel a hundred years younger. And my legs have stopped hurting at last," she laughed, turning up the volume on her old speakers with a jam-smeared hand. Right in the middle of her messy kitchen she let rip the wildest rock'n'roll I'd ever heard. 'Jailhouse Rock' lifted the preserve jars, making the glass rattle while Priska kept stoning apricots as she danced.

"Incredible! The scientific community must be informed!" I tried to make myself heard over the din but the dancer ignored me, ecstatically juggling apricots. Miss Priska was no longer Miss Priska. Neither was she lonely any longer. Her mailbox started to overflow. Neighbours wrote her indignant letters demanding that she respect their hours of rest and their privacy. She organised bizarre parties for seniors at which she served apricots in alcohol. Weird old men would turn up in her apartment. With their sideburns and backcombed hair they looked like actors from old Hollywood movies. One brought a saxophone and stayed till midnight playing the blues. "These are my new friends," Priska informed me in a conspiratorial whisper. "They just love apricot dumplings." Once I happened to lean out of the window and saw her new friends engaged in horseplay in an inflatable children's pool. They were wallowing in apricot mush. Stark naked.

"Miss Priscilla, please try at least not to play your music at full blast or you'll get yourself sectioned," I warned her, worn out by these antics. She just tilted her head back and shouted in abandon, "So what? Should I kill myself just because I feel like partying?"

I was getting seriously concerned about her. The changes in her behaviour, her unnatural rejuvenation and her deranged laughter convinced me that Miss Priska had succumbed to some mysterious mental illness. "Please, no more preserves. Please!" I implored. But she just kept stuffing apricots into my mouth.

One night I had a strange dream. I was standing in Priscilla's garden and felt my body getting bigger, swelling up and rounding out until I turned into a giant ball. My legs and arms disappeared and I was rolling towards the fringed tulips. My skin suddenly burst open, a weird yellow liquid seeping from what used to be my navel. I woke up with an overwhelming sense of disgust. The sweat-covered sheets and a bad premonition made me get up and walk down to Miss Priska's. I found the door to her flat open and the place empty. Music was playing in the living room crammed with bric-a-brac and Elvis's portraits. The plaintive tones of a Spanish guitar meandered among endless rows of jars. 'Love me tender, love me sweet,' sang the velvety voice and it was as if Presley were standing right there in the kitchen playing especially for her.

I went out into the garden. It was illuminated with striped paper lanterns and a full moon that was like an orange-coloured fizzy vitamin C tablet. Priscilla stood in the yellow light, stark naked. The long black hair cascading down her naked back reminded me of a flowing river. The skin on her body seemed to vibrate as if crawling with ants. "Priscilla!" I called out but the woman didn't respond. Suddenly she began to dance. Gently swaying to the sound of the guitar, she drew invisible signs in the air, swinging her hips lasciviously. She turned around. I gasped at her firm, rejuvenated, rhythmically swaying breasts. Her eyes were closed and her face bore the kind of expression you see in people who are about to leap to their death from the eighth floor. I felt goosebumps on my arms and a hard lump swelling in my throat. The naked woman danced slowly towards the apricot tree. And then she began to grow smaller. She kept shrinking and shrinking and before I could reach her, she had disappeared for good. The apricot tree had absorbed her at the very spot where she used to pour out the coffee dregs. By now there was no fruit on the tree, only peeling bark, black, as if scorched by fire. I noticed something crawling on the tree. A thousand tiny little girls sat on the blackened branches dangling their feet. They all wore fifties polka-dot dresses by Christian Dior. I noticed that all the miniature Miss Priskas were giggling about something.

One mini-Priska noticed me. As she pointed her finger at me all the other little girls fell silent. A thousand pairs of eyes bored into mine. The sweat pouring off me smelled of fear. "Miss Priska, what's happened to you?" I stammered. A sinister smile spread across their faces. "I'm not Priska," they squeaked in unison, "I'm Apricot," echoing each other in endless repetition. Their high-pitched voices kept getting louder and mingled with Elvis's song to the point where everything merged into an unbearable cacophony. I was in pain. Blood came streaming out of my ears, turning my pyjamas red. The little Apricots waved to me cheerfully. I ran off in terror.

Go Slow Therapy

I tripped over her, in the street, just like that. I was in a hurry to cross the road and then suddenly, crash-bang! My heels made a nasty screeching sound and I landed on my rear. She was teeny. Tinier than a garden gnome. She was wearing a hat with woollen bobbles of every hue. "Can't you look where you're going, are you blind or what?!" I fumed. The little woman grinned. I tried to get up but my legs refused to obey me. "Shit," I swore, trying to get my ankle to work. The woman giggled and shouted, "Go Slow Therapy!" I looked her in the eye: they were yellowish-brown, the colour of amber. She just laughed and shook her head, which made the bobbles on her hat jiggle up and down. She was weird. There was something weasel-like about her face. "What's that supposed to mean?" I asked, irritated. The dwarf woman wiped her nose in a huge chequered handkerchief. "Just wait and see," she said and disappeared. I looked around in astonishment, then got up and limped to the trolleybus stop. The bus came after a while and I got on. And that's when it all began.

I'm totally neurotic. I bite my fingernails and never have time for anything. I'm always in a hurry. Indecisive people, long conversations and slow lifts wind me up. Traffic jams on the way to work drive me into a blind frenzy and make me want to kick anyone in front of my trolleybus. I'm allergic to tourists asking for directions. I can't stand vacations and national holidays. I get worked up about children asking pointless questions. I suffer panic attacks and wake up in the middle of the night because of phone calls I didn't deal with during the day. I don't eat much and am often constipated. There's a strict inspector sitting inside of me. If she catches me not working hard enough she transmits harsh, reproachful signals to my brain. Sometimes she doesn't stop cracking her whip till late at night. I'm not a nice person to be with, I'm permanently angry and have every day planned out to the last second.

That's why that midget really got to me. I'll be late again. Tripping over wasn't part of my plan. Now my ankle hurts and the trolleybus is dawdling along like a worn-out old nag. And there's this irritating old lady with a blue rinse and an appalling wheelie bag. Twice she drove it over my feet. The red light takes forever to change and someone around here smells really bad. Nerves make my eyelids twitch as I studiously avoid looking at my watch. Suddenly a mobile starts to ring. The ringing gets louder and louder and I'm mentally cursing the deaf idiot who can't be bothered to pick up. "That wasn't nice of you," says a man in a grey coat turning to me as he slowly fishes his mobile out of his pocket. Every eye on the trolleybus is fixed on me and I realise I'm sweating even more profusely. "What's going on?" I snap in exasperation. A brunette with enormous artificial eyelashes smiles. "Go Slow Therapy."

"Have you gone crazy?" I ask, and the man with the mobile in his hand whispers, "It's just started."

The trolleybus reaches a stop. Everyone gets off. I realise I'm going to be seriously late for my meeting. I want to take my mobile out of my pocket but can't move my hands. My fingers are stiff, cold and gnarled. They're somebody else's hands, helplessly folded in my lap, refusing to obey me. I try to get up but my legs refuse to obey and I just sit there watching the trolleybus leave my stop. At first I'm gripped by helpless fury, which after twenty minutes turns to panic and finally into dull apathy. I'm the last person left on the bus. For some mysterious reason nobody gets on. Black Mamba from *Kill Bill* comes to my mind, flexing her fingers after she's recovered from a coma. I try to move one of my little fingers at least a fraction. The harder I try the stiffer it gets.

"I can't move!" I scream as the trolleybus arrives at the terminus. The driver pokes his head out of his cabin with a tired sigh. "Go Slow Therapy, huh?"

"What the hell does go slow therapy mean?" I yell back, by now thoroughly fed up with this phrase. "It does sometimes happen on this line," the man says, taking a sandwich out of his bag. "I don't know why. It's something to do with speed. At least that's what this lady said to me. The faster you think, talk, walk, breathe, the slower you get. You might even find that you stop moving altogether," he explains.

"OK, but what am I supposed to do now?" I ask, disgusted by the bits of salami dropping from his mouth. "Well," he replies, "they say you've got to start breathing slowly and properly and generally take it really, really slow."

"Breathe slowly, what sort of nonsense is that, there's nothing wrong with my breathing, I've being doing that since I was a baby, after all." Now I'm getting seriously worked up. At that moment I realise I can't move my head and my tongue is stiffening up. I mumble something.

"You see?" says the man, wiping his mouth on his sleeve. "You mustn't get worked up!" Then he proceeds to open a bottle of mineral water and drink it with gusto. "Slowly. That's how you'll have to do everything from now on," he says. "You'll have to learn how to walk slowly, look slowly, think slowly and above all, you mustn't try too hard. You mustn't push anything, especially not yourself. Good luck with it, and in the meantime you can stay here as long as you need!"

He closes his cabin door and starts the engine. The trolleybus sets off and I realise how hard this is. This slow breathing. I try to relax, forget about everything, try not to want anything and, above all, to stay completely calm. Every now and then the thought of something I have to do crowds in on my thoughts. My nerves are on edge. My stomach is in knots. The inspector inside me is tapping her pen impatiently. A meeting with a client. An interim activity report and a financial summary, a tax return, an order form to send out, a work meeting to arrange… The trolleybus has covered its route a million times and still I can't move.

"That's it for today!" the driver suddenly announces, pulling into the terminus. He collects his things and is about to get off. "Hey," I shout, "you can't leave me here like this! It's almost night and I still can't move!" The man scratches his head and says he can't help me. I'm the only one on this course of slow walking therapy. All he can offer is a warm blanket and what's left of his roll. "A course of therapy is a course of therapy." He shrugs his shoulders. "Last time, I had someone sitting here for a week until he managed to slow down." He gets off the trolleybus and waves good-bye. Has he gone crazy, I wonder? Or have I? The inspector inside me applies her most powerful lever – my conscience – but I can no longer weep. Even my tears are stuck somewhere beneath my eyelids.

I've been living on the trolleybus for two weeks now. The passengers are peculiar. The man I silently sent to hell because of his ringing mobile always greets me with a friendly smile. He's done this course of therapy, too. He used to be addicted to his phone. Apparently he wouldn't even go to the sauna without his mobile. The driver supplies me with bread rolls and whenever I'm able to open my mouth he pours a little water down my throat. The brunette with the enormous eyelashes teaches me how to breathe properly and the blue-rinsed old lady gives me massages to silence the inspector inside me.

The inspector has finally stopped cracking her whip. Today I'll be up to making my way to the back exit. I get off. I smell and look a bit like a bag lady. Never mind. I watch cars rush past and people walk by. It's not difficult. I inhale slowly until I feel a balloon inflating in my belly. I open my mouth slightly and exhale, slowly. The more slowly I breathe the slower my movements get. I place one foot on the pavement and, slowly shifting the weight of my body onto it, take a step forward. Slowly. I've got time. Time to look around. To take things in. Nothing matters except the movement itself. The way I walk. I am aware of the present. I am in the here and now. I notice a disabled woman's cane catch between the paving stones. A drunken old man dances in front of the presidential palace. A depressed Vietnamese in an Asian bistro gazes at its steamed-up window. A woman in lacquered pumps picks her nose. People are protesting outside the presidential palace, someone is on hunger strike. There are tramps and Romanian children begging. A blind accordion player, weeping. A crazy lady with an Alsatian in a sweater. People asleep on benches. Two men kissing. A woman jogging with headphones on. I notice details I've never noticed before. Grinning faces on a building's facade as well as a woman feeding an old ginger tomcat by a rubbish bin. I cross the road. Slowly. A shiny BMW steps on its brakes at the last minute. Its furious driver screams out of the window: "Are you asleep, you stupid cow?!" I grin and say nothing. A tiny little woman is dancing on the car hood. She is smaller than a garden gnome. Multi-coloured woollen bobbles dance on her enormous hat. She is singing. "Go Slow Therapy, param-pam-pam, Go Slow…"

Sea Anemone

Her studio resembles a stinking airtight can. Miss Annemarie hasn't opened her windows in years. Keeping the heavy curtains drawn night and day has solved the cleaning problem once and for all. She can't stand big clean-ups, blasts of fresh air, or noise. She can't stand anything remotely resembling change. That's why she's kept her flat in the same state since spotting a luxurious set of modular furniture in the window of a store in 1971. She grabbed her cheque book and, without batting an eyelid, coughed up an unheard-of amount for the joys of modern design.

"Your place stinks like some sleazy bar, shouldn't I let some fresh air in?" I ask, as always, setting a carrier with a special meal for her gall-bladder diet on the kitchen counter. Annemarie lifts the lid on the metal container with her index finger. "Vegetable soup—not again," she grumbles, wiping the vinyl tablecloth with a dishcloth of indeterminate colour.

That smell is truly a mystery. The place stinks as if she smoked two packs a day, even though she claims never to have touched a cigarette. "No point opening the window. It comes from me," she says hoarsely as I struggle to open the window. "What comes from you?" I ask, baffled.

Instead of replying, the old woman lumbers over to a chest of drawers and produces a photograph. "The smoke, my dear, the smoke." She makes me sit in a rickety armchair and shoves a black-and-white photograph in my face. "Have a look," she says.

Fascinated, I examine a curvaceous woman in a silver bikini with tassels. Shell-shaped bra cups cling to her breasts and her head is adorned with a curious headband reminiscent of coral reefs. She is grinning broadly, holding a cigar in one hand. "Is that you?" I ask, my jaw dropping. Miss Annemarie straightens up as far as her ancient body permits and declares proudly, "Sea Anemone. A number I performed for five years in Prague's top striptease joint!"

My confused look wanders from the sexy creature in the photograph to Miss Annemarie's sallow, wrinkled face, and back. "But this proves that you used to smoke," I say suspiciously, making Annemarie crack up and slap her thighs. "I did smoke. . . but with what, my dear, with what!" she laughs, snatching the photo away to examine it under the fringed lamp that must have once been a pristine white.

"Those were the days," she sighs in delight. "And the money! It just came rolling in! Our club used to put on the finest shows—we were compared to the Moulin Rouge!" Her face is radiant and I notice a hint of the flirtatiousness that I detected in the youthful photograph.

"So what happened to it?" I say with a smile, going to the kitchen to warm up her lunch.

"Oh, you know. The Party closed it down after 1968, saying the petty bourgeoisie undermined the orderly life of the working people. So I got a job in a meat-processing factory."

I put out the cutlery, serve the warmed-up soup, and call out to Miss Annemarie, who is reliving her Sea Anemone stunt with her eyes fixed on the grubby closed curtains. The old lady gingerly pads over to the table and begins to eat. She grumbles about the fat-free gall-bladder diet and reminisces about the spicy sausages she used to devour at the meat-processing factory. "And you see, this is how low I've sunk now. I stink like an ashtray and my gall bladder is done in."

She leaves bits of boiled broccoli on the side of the plate, saying she wouldn't eat that stuff if they burned her alive. I dust her plastic flowers while she cuts up some boiled fish with trembling hands. I offer to vacuum but Miss Annemarie stops me indignantly, saying the vacuum cleaner only stirs up the dust. Besides, her place is clean and she's never needed a maid.

"But you have me as your home help," I object, but she just shakes her head, indicating it's all the same to her.

When she is done, I wash the dishes, and while I collect her dirty laundry Miss Annemarie gets ready for her afternoon nap. She sits on the bed, thoughtfully combing her long, once-gorgeous hair. I watch her for a while. Miss Annemarie stares at me with her short-sighted, watery eyes. Putting the hairbrush down she says, "Good night." I tell her I'll bring her laundry back when I come with her lunch the next day, but the old lady is already snoring away.

I slam the door and finally breathe in some fresh air unpolluted by smoke. Then I take her laundry to the Geriatric Centre. The woman who works there will separate the underwear from the socks. Everything will be neatly washed, dried, and packed into a plastic bag with 'Annemarie' written on it in black marker.

The next day, as soon as I turn the key, the powerful stench of cigarette smoke hits my nose. I can barely see through the permanent twilight of the room. Miss Annemarie is lying silent in the unmade bed, just as I left her the day before. "Good morning!" I call out, my voice heavy with irony, and then notice that something is not quite right. Something that makes me walk slowly over to the old lady before I put down my bag, something that makes the hairs on the back of my neck stand on end.

Putting my load down, I gently place the palm of my hand on her chest. The old lady is not breathing. Her mouth is open and her dry eyes are staring at the closed curtains. I sit down in the rickety armchair and switch on the light. I take out my mobile.

I notice strange bluish smoke emanating from the dead woman's body. Rising quietly, the smoke drifts along the ceiling before descending again. Next to the dead woman's body it curls into the shape of a woman with a cigar in her hand and a coral headband. The smoke woman sits on the bed, watching me quietly. She has the full lips and face of the young Miss Annemarie of the photograph. We eye each other. She smiles flirtatiously.

The woman, or rather the smoke, suddenly begins to undulate, spreading her legs wide to give a posthumous demonstration of her Sea Anemone act. My eyes begin to sting. I cough violently. I get up from the armchair and yank open the jammed window at my first attempt. The smoke-Annemarie gives a shiver. She casts a mournful look at the body on the bed. She draws on the cigar once more before the draught sucks her through the open window, out into the street.